"I'll pick you u
date."

"Okay." She tucked a loosened strand of blond hair behind her ear.

He followed the motion of her hand, his heart beating rapidly. Should he trust his first impressions of Evy Shaw? Sweet, smart, very pretty. Was his initial instinct about her correct?

"You don't have to wait for me, Charlie."

"Of course I do. I'll walk you to your car."

She slung the purse strap over her shoulder. "Another Southern-gentleman thing?"

He followed Evy to the front door. "So let me be one, okay? And for the record, I *want* to walk you to your car."

Evy worried her bottom lip between her teeth as she set the alarm. He stuffed his hands into his pockets. Before he did something stupid.

Suppose he was wrong about Evy? Could she be hiding behind a mask, the image she wanted him to see? And if so, why?

Who was the real Evy Shaw? Was seeing believing in her case?

Maybe… Maybe not. Only time would tell.

Lisa Carter and her family make their home in North Carolina. In addition to her Love Inspired novels, she writes romantic suspense for Abingdon Press. When she isn't writing, Lisa enjoys traveling to romantic locales, teaching writing workshops and researching her next exotic adventure. She has strong opinions on barbecue and ACC basketball. She loves to hear from readers. Connect with Lisa at lisacarterauthor.com.

Books by Lisa Carter

Love Inspired

Coast Guard Courtship
Coast Guard Sweetheart
Falling for the Single Dad
The Deputy's Perfect Match

The Deputy's Perfect Match

Lisa Carter

LOVE INSPIRED BOOKS

Recycling programs
for this product may
not exist in your area.

ISBN-13: 978-0-373-89918-0

The Deputy's Perfect Match

www.Harlequin.com

Printed in U.S.A.

Is there no balm in Gilead? Is there no physician there? Why then has the health of the daughter of my people not been restored?
—*Jeremiah 8:22*

Dedicated to Billy & Kathy Davis—
thanks for your friendship over the years.

This book is also dedicated to those separated
from people they love by circumstances outside
their control. May you truly find the balm of
Gilead and may the years the locusts have eaten
be restored a hundredfold in your life
as if those hard years had never been.

Acknowledgments

Thanks to Janet Morley and the
library specialists—Brandy Hamilton,
Daphne McLawhorn, Trish Preston—
at the East Regional Library for taking me
through "a day in the life of a librarian."
Thanks to Sonny, who strolled into the library
that morning and allowed me to "practice" issuing
him a pretend library card. It was so much fun
pretending to walk in Evy's shoes—ahem,
high heels. Any errors are, of course, my own.

I've taken a few literary liberties with the
sheriff's department for the sake of the story line.
I hold all of you at the highest regard
for the challenging yet essential work you
perform every day on our behalf.

A big thank-you to the dedicated men and women
of the Accomack County Sheriff's Department,
and to deputies everywhere for their
commitment to serve and protect.

Chapter One

In the corner booth of the Sandpiper Café, Accomack County Deputy Sheriff Charlie Pruitt stared at the three Duer sisters.

"Let me get this straight—you want me to arrest the new Kiptohanock librarian?"

Watercolor artist Amelia Scott fidgeted on the cracked green vinyl upholstery. "Not arrest. Investigate."

Her sister, Caroline Clark, nodded. "Technically speaking, Miss Shaw hasn't broken any laws."

Charlie raised one eyebrow. "Then technically speaking, this sounds like a waste of taxpayer dollars and the department's manpower."

Amelia moistened her lips. "We're asking you, as an old family friend, for a favor."

His attention cut to the youngest sister, sandwiched between Amelia and Caroline. She'd been uncharacteristically silent during the morning meeting. Everyone in Kiptohanock had always believed he and his childhood sweetheart, Honey Duer, would marry one day.

Everyone, including him. Until a certain Coast Guardsman by the name of Sawyer Kole arrived on the Eastern Shore four years ago. Charlie had been cast aside like yesterday's fish guts.

Until Sawyer Kole abruptly left the Shore. Then Charlie played the fool by taking up with Honey Duer again. When Kole returned as suddenly as he'd left, once more Charlie had been jettisoned from Honey's life like so much flotsam.

He grimaced. Charlie was all too aware that in the love department, the town of Kiptohanock considered him a laughingstock.

Charlie grabbed his regulation hat off the seat beside him. "If we're done here—"

"Something's not right about that woman." Honey placed her hands on the sticky linoleum tabletop. "She's hiding something."

The fluorescent lighting caught the sparkle in the diamond ring on Honey's finger. He squared his shoulders. Honey was lost to him forever. She was now Sawyer Kole's wife and pregnant with their first child.

Past time for Charlie to move on with his life.

But so far, he had only his career. And law enforcement didn't come close to soothing the raw, empty places Honey's absence left in his life.

Strapped in the stroller beside the booth, Amelia's nine-month-old son, Patrick, let out a wail.

Amelia fumbled through a diaper bag and handed Patrick a cracker. "We're living on borrowed time, girls. Nap time awaits." The baby made smacking noises as he gummed the cracker.

"Why do you think the librarian is hiding something?" Charlie fixed each of the sisters with his most intimidating look. "Has she done or said something to make you feel threatened?"

Caroline's gaze flitted toward the plate-glass window overlooking the town square. "She hasn't exactly said anything…"

He crossed his arms over his brown uniform. "What *has* she done to raise your suspicions?"

Amelia fiddled with packets of sweetener. "She's always hanging around our family. Trying to insinuate herself. She insisted on helping Daddy grill hot dogs for the Fourth of July cookout. And she wanted to be *my* nursery helper during Vacation Bible School in June, but not help Miss Pauline's second-grade class."

He rolled his tongue in his cheek. "Right.

'Cause such civic and church behaviors are so often warning signs for deeper, deviant issues."

Caroline glared. "You need to get serious about this, Charlie."

"*You three* need to get serious. Ever think maybe you have overactive imaginations?" He blew a breath between his lips. "Or a paranoia complex?"

Amelia shook her head. "I thought the same as you, Charlie. That Honey was imagining things, until I started noticing the librarian's behavior. She has a way of almost disappearing into the background. Then suddenly you realize she's been there listening the whole time."

Charlie fought for patience. "Why am I not surprised this originated with Honey?"

Honey's eyebrows arched. "Are you implying I'm a drama queen?"

"If the pearls fit…" He shrugged.

Caroline bit back a smile. "Be that as it may, Honey's right. Once she expressed her concern, I noticed how Miss Shaw is always studying the Duers. Not staring at the Colonnas or the Turners. Just us."

He frowned. "Like a stalker?"

"She watches us." Honey folded her hands over her rounded abdomen. "Especially Sawyer."

"This is about…?" Charlie hardened his heart.

"I'm outta here." He began easing out of the booth.

"Miss Shaw watches all of us," Honey said. "Sawyer most of all. But not in a romantic way. It's just strange. And it scares me." Her brown eyes misted. "Please, Charlie. We were friends once…"

He stilled. Friends…when he'd hoped for so much more. But old loyalty to Honey warred with his better judgment.

"I cannot utilize official resources without legal justification."

Caroline leaned forward. "But unofficially, could you make inquiries? At least talk to her?"

"You want me to spy on her?" His voice rose. "Seriously?"

Caroline's mouth thinned. "Just get to know her. Find out what she's after."

Amelia lifted her chin. "Honey's seven months pregnant, Charlie. She doesn't need this kind of stress in her life."

Honey's lips trembled. "Please, Charlie…"

Charlie raked his hand over his head. "An unofficial investigation only. I'll nose around. See what I learn."

Amelia and Caroline exchanged relieved looks.

Honey smiled. "Thank you, Charlie."

"And if I find nothing suspicious…" He motioned in the general direction of the Kiptohanock library. "You'll let go of this, and leave the poor woman alone."

"Why sure, Charlie boy." Amelia winked at Caroline. "We'll welcome her with open arms to our little fishing hamlet. Give her the same warm red-carpet treatment we give every 'come here."

"You do that." He edged out of the booth. "'Cause I'd sure hate to have to lock three Kiptohanock mothers in the county jail."

Charlie made a show of placing his hat upon his head. "Not that I'm afraid to arrest the three of you Duers. I'm thinking more about the safety of the other inmates."

Before the ladies could protest, he threw down enough bills to cover the price of coffee and Long John doughnuts. The lingering aromas of ham, fried potatoes and pancakes followed him across the crowded diner.

He yanked open the glass door in a whoosh of air. With a jingle of bells, he exited the café to do his duty. Which promised to be about as much fun as being Tasered.

Charlie shot a swift look at his watch. He'd have to hurry. No telling when the next call would come from Dispatch.

The cawing of seagulls vied with the sounds of water lapping against the town docks. The scent of brine filled his nostrils as he made his way past the gazebo on the square.

On the wide-planked steps of the brick Victorian that housed the library, he pivoted for one final look at his patrol cruiser in the parking lot of the Sandpiper. Out of habit, he surveyed the town.

The narrow Delmarva Peninsula—composed of portions of Delaware, Maryland and Virginia—separated the Chesapeake Bay and mainland from the Atlantic Ocean. The fishing village of Kiptohanock, Virginia lay seaside.

A white clapboard church hugged the Kiptohanock shoreline. Its steeple pierced the blue sky. Recreational and commercial fishing boats bobbed in the harbor.

Charlie's gaze skimmed past the post office. The outfitter and boat repair shops. In the gentle sea breeze, flags fluttered outside the Coast Guard station. Emanating from the village green like spokes on a wheel, gingerbread-trimmed homes meandered down leaf-canopied lanes.

Home. It was his job to do everything in his power to protect Kiptohanock and the people who resided here. Including assess the threat level of a librarian?

Charlie removed his hat and grunted. Talk about fool's errands. Swinging the stout oak door open wide, he ventured inside the cool interior. He waited in the high-ceilinged foyer and allowed his eyes to adjust from the bright glare of the midmorning sunshine to the more subdued lighting of the library.

No one manned the librarian's desk at the base of the curving mahogany staircase. The cushy grouping of chairs also remained empty. From brief forays on behalf of long-ago high school projects, Charlie remembered that upstairs lay the fiction and science rooms.

He wasn't fond of books. Nor was the library one of his favorite places. These days, once off duty and motionless, he went to sleep.

But he doubted much had changed in the library after old Mrs. Beal retired a few months ago. Nothing in Kiptohanock ever changed much. Which was exactly why he liked it here.

To the right, the oak-paneled room contained the reference section and a bank of desks topped by computer screens. But to the left, the soft murmur of voices drew him forward. Where he discovered chest-high bookshelves surrounding an open area with a large green rug.

A cluster of kids hunched over a book with a fierce dog on the cover. One of the children turned the page. There were giggles. The blonde child in the center of the group glanced up as his shadow fell across them.

The blonde child passed the book to Caroline Clark's new stepdaughter, "I didn't hear you come in." The blonde rose in a fluid motion.

He blinked. She wasn't a child. Just a very small, blonde adult. This five-foot nothing waif was the person shadowing the Duer family?

At six-foot-three, Charlie towered over the petite blonde. "*You're* the new librarian?"

She tilted her head to meet his gaze. Her wheat-colored ponytail danced across her shoulders. "Yes, I am."

In a glance, she took him in—from his creased khaki uniform trousers to the tie adorning his short-sleeved summer uniform shirt to his dark hair. And finally coming to rest upon the tan hat he carried in his hands.

Behind her black horn-rimmed glasses, her large blue eyes appeared owlish. Uncertainty flickered. "Can I help you, Officer? Is there a problem?"

He stared at her. The cork-soled wedges. The white denim capris. The fluttery candy-pink top.

This wisp of a creature was the Kiptohanock Stalker? He could probably encircle the librarian's waist with both his hands and have room to spare.

"Is there a book I can help you find?"

Her voice was soft, as befitted a librarian, he supposed. And sort of sweet.

Charlie realized his mouth was agape. He closed it. "I don't read."

Guileless as a child, her sky-blue eyes widened. "Oh… I'm so sorry, but we offer a program for that. I'd be glad to help if you're willing to put in the time."

Unlike the Tidewater brogue Kiptohanockians spoke, she had one of those accents from anywhere and nowhere. Thanks to television, like most of America.

Then what she'd said registered with Charlie. And what he'd actually said to her first.

"I didn't mean I don't know *how* to read." He shuffled his regulation shoes on the rug. "I meant that books are not for me."

Pink tinted her pale features. "Of course you read. You're a sheriff."

In his line of work, he couldn't remember the last time he'd seen a woman blush. He hadn't been sure women still did. But the rosy spots of color brought the librarian's face to life.

She wasn't wearing makeup. To her credit, maybe she wasn't a vain woman. She could have done much more with her appearance than she did, matter of fact.

Thank you, Honey Duer Kole, for yet another wild-goose chase. This was ridiculous. He was ridiculous. And Honey was certifiable. The little blonde cleared her throat.

He shook himself. Not like him to blank out. Law enforcement officers were apt to end their careers—and their lives—if not always on the alert. Time to beat an apologetic retreat and get back to real work.

"I'm not the sheriff. I'm just a deputy." Hat in hand, he turned on his heel and headed toward the door. "Thanks anyway, ma'am. Perhaps another time."

No mystery nor Mata Hari here.

The front door opened, but something made Charlie glance over his shoulder. In time to see the librarian's face change. As Caroline Duer Clark crossed the threshold.

When aquatic veterinarian, Caroline Clark, sauntered into the library, Evy Shaw made herself as unobtrusive as possible behind the desk. Which was not a problem for Evy. She was used to fading into the woodwork.

Or in her case, fading into the bookshelves. She often wore her invisibility like a Romulan cloaking device.

She winced. Best to keep that bit of geekiness under wraps. Her passion for all things *Star Trek* didn't exactly cause men to line up at her door.

Nine-year-old Izzie Clark bounced up from the reading rug. "Mom, you'll love the books I got this week for us to read together."

Caroline's eyes softened at the sight of her stepdaughter. Evy had arrived in town a few weeks before Caroline returned to her estranged family. Caroline and Weston Clark's romance first began in the library. And through a series of events involving sea creatures, Caroline, Weston and Izzie found their happily-ever-after with each other in a restored lighthouse.

Evy bit back a sigh. Minus the fairy-tale ending, she and Caroline had far more in common than the oldest Duer sister imagined.

There was a brief flurry of activity as parents started arriving. The children in the oceanside fishing community brought much-needed excitement not only to the library but also to Evy's life. She loved children. And story hour was the highlight of her week.

"Goodbye, Miss Shaw." Izzie waved. "See you next week." The solid oak door shut with a decisive click.

Someone cleared a throat. Evy nearly launched into outer space and grabbed hold of the counter. Who—

A pair of piercing hazel eyes studied her. The dark-haired, broad-shouldered young deputy. She'd forgotten him while dealing with the Duer sister. This unaccustomed subterfuge was playing havoc with her nerves.

She put a shaky hand to her throat. With his

height and build, the deputy was a former high
school or college football player. Probably both.
He'd be intimidating to someone on the wrong
side of the law.

Or someone with something to hide. Like her.
On a quest to find her long-lost brother.

When he'd placed the Smokey Bear hat on
his head earlier, he'd been on his way out the
door. Until Caroline Clark arrived. The hat—
Evy craned her neck—added another five inches
to his already imposing stature.

"Can I help you, Deputy?"

He removed the hat. The muscles underneath
his fitted uniform shirt flexed. Her attention
skittered. Did he wear a Kevlar vest? How dangerous was the life of a deputy sheriff in peaceful Kiptohanock?

Mind your own business, Evy.

The deputy positioned the hat next to a stack
of books on her desk. "I need a library card."

"I thought you didn't…"

He raised an eyebrow.

"I mean, you don't seem the type to…"

He folded his arms across his chest. Which,
for her, was eye level. His gold badge gleamed
in the light of the green banker's lamp atop her
desk. Deputy Sheriff, Accomack County, it read.

"Is getting a library card going to be a problem, Miss… Miss…?"

"Shaw. Evangeline Shaw." Was it suddenly hot in here or just her? "Getting a card will not be a problem, Deputy."

"It's Deputy Pruitt." Hand extended, he reached across the counter. "Charles Everett Pruitt the Third."

Her eyes flitted to his hand.

The deputy's gaze caught hers and held steady. "I find it amazing that in as small a place as Kiptohanock, our paths haven't crossed until now."

She took his hand. His hand engulfed hers. Her heart stutter-stepped at the touch of his strong, warm fingers against her skin.

"Pleased to meet you," she whispered.

Why was she whispering? Goose bumps tingled up and down her arm.

His lantern jaw tightened. Frowning, he extracted his hand from hers.

She angled toward the monitor and hit a button on the keyboard. "There are a few questions for you to answer on the application."

"Fire away." He crossed his arms again, tucking his hands out of sight beneath impressive biceps. "I meant that in a figurative sense, mind you." His lips twitched.

She'd always liked men with a sense of—

Evy jerked her eyes to the screen. "Name? Oh." She swallowed. "You told me already."

She concentrated on typing the information. "Pruitt... Charles—"

"Friends call me Charlie."

She stopped midkeystroke. Was that an invitation to be his friend, or was the deputy just being chatty? He didn't strike Evy as the chatty sort.

"Address?" She was whispering again...

He rattled off an address belonging to one of the Victorian homes on a side street close to the town square.

The deputy unfolded his arms and planted his elbows on the wooden counter. "And how about you?"

Evy's mouth went dry. The corded muscles of his forearms gave her pause.

He leaned toward Evy. "Where do you live, Miss Shaw? Turnabout is fair play, don't you think?"

With his chiseled countenance, Mr. Law Enforcement bore a striking resemblance to Clark Kent aka Superman. He'd probably be very handsome if he ever relaxed his rigid features. With effort, she wrenched her gaze to the computer.

She poised her fingers over the keyboard. "I'm boarding with Pauline Crockett off Seaside Road. Near—"

"I'm familiar with Miss Pauline's farm."

"You're a 'been here then. Isn't that what the locals call themselves?" She focused on the screen. "Which makes me a 'come here. What's your telephone number?"

"Why? Are you planning to ask me out, Miss Shaw?"

Her heart palpitated. She was unused to—and unsettled by—the oh-so-masculine attention.

She gestured at the computer. "It's for th-the form."

He laughed. "Turnabout is fair play, remember, Miss Shaw?"

She pointed at a tray of business cards with the library's website and phone number. "I think I have enough information to process the application."

Was he flirting with her? Or mocking her? She lifted her chin.

He straightened, his hazel eyes going serious. "I didn't mean to… I thought we—"

"It will take me a minute to create the card. If you can't stick around, I'll mail it to you."

He shuffled his big feet. "I can wait."

"In the meantime…" She shoved a welcome folder at him. "Here's information about the services available at the library. And a schedule of upcoming events."

She gave him a nice view of her back. Better to get this over with ASAP. "In the packet are the conditions and privileges granted to you as a borrower." She worked quickly to laminate the card.

With the card hot off the machine, she faced him once again. "I should've asked for your ID first. Saved you the trouble of answering unnecessary questions. But per library regulations, I'm going to have to see some picture identification."

A muscle ticking in his jaw, Mr. Law Enforcement fished his wallet out of his pocket. He extracted his license and passed it to her. She skimmed it for a split second.

She pushed his new library card and his license across the counter. "Here's your card." The less contact, the better.

Mr. Law Enforcement had a curious effect on her nerve endings. "There is a one-dollar replacement fee if you lose the card."

"I won't lose it." The deputy inserted the cards into his wallet. "I don't lose things I go after."

She opened her mouth, thought better of it and clamped her lips together.

He smiled.

She caught the edge of the desk. The flash of those even, white teeth could blind a person. When he smiled like that, his stern countenance became almost handsome.

Evy placed her palms flat against the wood

to steady herself. No *almost* about it. Deputy Charles Everett Pruitt the Third was quite handsome.

Heart-throbbingly handsome. He should smile more often. She wondered why he didn't. Not that he and his smile—or lack thereof—were any of her business.

That was the problem with small towns like Kiptohanock. Especially small Southern towns. Everybody was into everybody else's business. And the nosiness appeared to be contagious. She needed—to quote the stalwart Captain Kirk—to raise her shields.

Maybe local law enforcement made it a point to get to know newcomers. But Evy couldn't afford anyone prying into her background. Not when she had so many secrets to keep.

When Evangeline Shaw's expression transformed at the sight of Caroline, Charlie's instincts kicked into gear. With her guileless blue eyes not so guileless anymore, he'd changed his mind about leaving the library.

Maybe the Duer sisters weren't as off base in their suspicions as he'd imagined. Something was going on with the librarian.

He witnessed firsthand the melding thing the Duer sisters insisted she did with people. Practically blending into the background. Undercover agents could have learned a trick or two from the quiet librarian.

Exiting the library with Izzie chattering non-stop, Caroline did an admirable job of not blowing his so-called cover.

So he'd invented the need for a library card. Any excuse to justify his continued presence in Miss Shaw's hallowed hall of books. But he'd embarrassed her with his mild stab at flirtatiousness.

Either she wasn't the sort of girl who played games or, worse, he'd lost his appeal to women since Honey. Maybe Miss Shaw wasn't into his type. Not every woman liked a guy in uniform.

"Was that everything you needed, Deputy?"

It hadn't escaped his notice she'd misdirected his attempts to call him by name. He found her reticence intriguing. He found the touch of her hand disturbing.

Which might have been the most troublesome warning sign of all.

"I—I…" His gaze darted around the reception area. Searching for a reason to see her again. On behalf of the investigation, of course.

Charlie jabbed his finger at the purple poster tacked on the wall behind the librarian. "I want to register for the book club."

Her brow puckered. "What book club?" As if unsure of his meaning. Or stalling.

"Do you have other book clubs?"

"No…only this one, which meets every Thursday night."

"Then that's the one I want to join." He widened his stance, hips even with his feet. "It says you're the facilitator."

She turned and scanned the notice as if not trusting her memory. "Yes, I guess it does."

"Okay then."

She blinked.

"What do I need to do for Thursday? Just show up?"

She pursed her lips. Beautiful lips, he decided.

He scowled. *Stick to the case, Pruitt.*

Evangeline Shaw nudged her glasses higher onto the bridge of her nose. "Showing up is the least of what we do in the book club, Deputy Pruitt."

She gave him a prim look he remembered an English teacher or two bestowing on him during high school a decade ago. "You need to read the book first. With today being Monday, I'm not sure you'd be able—"

"You don't think I can read a book in three days, Miss Shaw?"

He also decided to make it his personal goal to be on a first-name basis with Miss Shaw and vice versa by Thursday.

"I don't know if this particular book selection…" Again with the blush.

She wound a strand of her hair around her finger. "I mean, I don't think this book would be your cup of tea."

He grinned. "Good thing the only tea I drink is sweet."

The blush deepened, and she stepped sideways. Barricading herself behind the stack of books?

He rubbed his chin. "How bad could it be? It's not *War and Peace*, is it?"

"No…not exactly." She toyed with the gold chain dangling around her neck. "It is a classic. Not your kind of book."

Charlie cocked his head. "I wouldn't be too sure about that, Miss Shaw, seeing as we barely know each other. Yet."

Her eyebrows rose.

Charlie's cell suddenly warbled.

The librarian's eyes narrowed. "Is that the theme to…?" She hummed a few bars.

His turn to flush, he pried the cell out of his pocket. Caller ID indicated Caroline Clark's home number.

Those Duer sisters. Couldn't even wait for him to get out of the line of fire before they wanted a report. He'd had police academy sergeants less demanding. He clicked the phone off.

She propped her elbows on the desk. *"Bonanza?"*

"I liked Westerns as a kid. Still do." He waited for the usual derisive comments.

Instead, she favored him with a genuine smile. And his gut flip-flopped.

"Me, too, Deputy." She motioned toward the second story. "We have an entire section devoted to Western historicals."

"Is that what the book club is reading this week?"

She fluttered her lashes. "Why no, it's not."

From underneath the counter, she drew out a thick, heavy paperback and plunked it in front of him. "This week we're reading and discussing another classic."

She smirked. "Welcome to the Jane Austen Reading Club, Deputy."

Chapter Two

Tuesday evening, Evy was just about to lock up when—

"I'm in over my head, Miss Shaw."

Evy shrieked. The key dropped out of her hand and fell with a clatter onto the library porch. Spinning around, she fell into the doorframe.

Stooping, Deputy Charlie Pruitt retrieved the key lying between their feet. "Sorry. Are you okay?"

Her breath came in short spurts, and she clutched the strap of her purse. "No thanks to you. You nearly gave me a heart attack."

The deputy nudged the brim of his hat higher onto his forehead. "I thought you saw me through the window when you set the alarm." His brow creased. "You're a nervous sort of gal, aren't you?"

She drew herself to her full height—all five feet three inches. "When somebody creeps up on you in the dark? You bet I am."

"I didn't creep up on you." He handed her the brass key. "And it isn't dark."

"Not yet." She fisted the key. "The sidewalks here roll up at five o'clock. Anyone would be nervous."

"Depends on what you're used to, I suppose." His eyebrow rose. "Kiptohanock's a pretty safe place. Where was it again you said you were from?"

Her mouth tightened. "I didn't say." She stuffed the key into a voluminous tote bag.

"So you didn't."

Arms folded across his chest, he leaned against one of the brick pillars bookending the veranda steps. His long legs blocked her exit. Or did she mean, her escape?

"Was there something I could help you with, Deputy?" She gestured at the darkened building. "As you can see, the library is closed."

She tapped her foot against the wide-planked boards. "Or are you stopping by to let me know you've decided to drop out of the book club?"

He smiled.

Evy's heart ratcheted up.

"Actually, Miss Shaw, I did want to talk to you about the book club."

"I'd be glad to return the book so you don't have to make another trip." She took a step toward him. "Did you leave it in your patrol car?" He didn't take the hint to move out of her way.

His smile, if anything, grew wider. "I appreciate the personal service—"

She flushed.

"—but I'm not dropping out of the book club. On the contrary, I've managed to read through the novel twice."

"Twice? Really?"

Charlie Pruitt broadened his shoulders and removed his hat. Which he placed over his heart.

Her heart did a minuet.

"Fact is, Miss Shaw, there are a few parts I'm having trouble digesting, and I wondered if you'd be willing to give me a few pointers so I'll be prepared for book club on Thursday."

"I'm— I..."

"How about over Chinese at the Four Corners Shopping Center?" He gave her a crooked smile. "I'm on my dinner break."

Suddenly the space between them felt extremely intimate. As if there weren't enough oxygen. Was he asking her out?

Of course not. He was asking for her help, her expertise. She was unused to male attention. Especially from someone so... She bit her lip. So male.

His mouth drooped. "You're probably too busy. I didn't mean to impose." He ducked his head. "Or presume."

She caught hold of his uniform sleeve. "I'm not busy."

His eyes snapped to her face.

Evy let go of his arm. Could she have sounded more pathetic? "I'm mean, I'm never too busy for a library patron."

Now she sounded like a cross between Mary Poppins and Margaret Thatcher. "I mean… might as well. We've both got to eat."

Stop talking. She closed her eyes. *Just stop talking.*

"Great."

She opened her eyes to find those long-lashed hazel eyes of his smiling at her. Her heart did a tango.

By sheer willpower, she dragged her gaze to the cleft in his chin. Maybe not a safe place to settle, either. Another blush mounted from beneath the collar of her white blouse.

"I'm an old-fashioned chow mein guy. How about you?"

She realized he was talking again. To her. "Umm… I like sweet and sour."

"Of course you do." He swept his hat across the length of the steps. "I'll follow you there, Miss Shaw."

"A police escort?" She smoothed the cuff of her blue cardigan and gathered her wits. "Should I be nervous?"

His eyes glinted. "Only if you've got something to hide."

The deputy's words felt like a kick in the gut. She quivered on the edge of the step. Perhaps this was a bad idea.

Hands in his pockets, he waited for her at the curb beside his patrol cruiser. But dinner—even dutch treat—with Deputy Pruitt proved too alluring a prospect for Evy to refuse. Law enforcement had to be suspicious by nature. It was probably nothing personal.

She hurried down the steps to her car and contemplated her next move. It might be smart to open up a tad. Allay any misgivings the deputy might have regarding a Kiptohanock newcomer. Disarm and distract.

And what better way to disarm and distract than a Regency-era book discussion?

In the alcove booth, Charlie edged back from the table. "You're a total purist, aren't you?" Aromas of soy sauce and stir-fry permeated the restaurant.

Evangeline Shaw paused midbite.

She gave him a sidelong look from beneath the eyelashes brushing her cheekbones. "What do you mean?" She lowered her chopsticks to the placemat adorned with Chinese characters.

"From classical literature to those." His eyes cut to her eating utensils.

"Oh." She swallowed. "Habit, I guess. Our housekeeper was Chinese, and when we went into the city, she always took me with her to visit her relatives in Chinatown."

He pursed his lips. "So they owned a restaurant?"

The librarian pushed the plate away. "What was your question about the book, Deputy?"

"The two most famous Chinatowns being in New York and San Francisco." He locked eyes with her. "But you don't sound like a New Yorker."

Evangeline Shaw held his gaze. "That's because I'm not from New York."

"So you call California home?"

The librarian lifted her chin. "As much as anywhere else, I suppose, Deputy Pruitt."

"Please, I insist you call me Charlie. It's the polite Kiptohanock way."

He took a sip of the hot green tea and made a face. "This would be better with sugar." He allowed a slow smile to spread across his face. "Everything's better with sugar, don't you think, Miss Shaw?"

Charlie enjoyed watching the librarian squirm

in the seat across from him. He waited a beat before adding, "Or may I call you Evangeline since we've broken egg rolls together?"

Her lips quirked as if she fought the urge to laugh.

Maybe he hadn't lost his touch, after all. "Were you a military brat?"

"No."

Charlie held his breath, hoping she'd open up. Just a little. A little was all he'd need to get this investigation underway.

Her cherry-red Mini Cooper already sported Virginia plates. No help there. But he memorized the license number in the parking lot in case he ever needed it.

She took a breath and exhaled. "My parents are tenured English professors at Stanford."

"Hence, I'm guessing, your early and lifelong love affair with books."

She twisted the paper napkin in her lap. "That must seem lame to someone like you."

He bristled. "What do you mean, 'someone like me'?"

She motioned toward the badge pinned to his uniform. "You are a self-admitted nonreader, Deputy Pruitt. I'm guessing, a man of action."

"My name is Charlie."

"Why join the book club, Charlie? *Pride and Prejudice* isn't exactly on most guys' top-ten lists." She arched her eyebrow. "If they even like to read. Which you made clear from the get-go that you did not."

The diminutive librarian possessed a bit of steel. Good to know.

He crossed his arms over his chest. "I'm trying to keep a promise."

She looked at him over the rim of her glasses.

"To expand my horizons. Jane Austen doesn't have to be only chick lit, you know. There's a lot in there for guys, too."

Her eyes narrowed. "Like what?" A literary gauntlet.

"Like...like..." He racked his brain for what he'd digested from his middle-of-the-night, off-duty incursions into Austenland.

She drummed her fingers on the table.

"Like a strong man doesn't have to be afraid of a strong woman like Elizabeth Bennet." Challenge accepted. "And it's funny, too."

She scowled. "In what way?"

"Her dad cracks jokes all the time." Charlie rested his elbows on the table. "Any dude surrounded by all those women would have to see the hilarious side of life or go insane."

"Oh, really?"

"You got any brothers and sisters?"

The librarian hesitated. "It's just me and my parents."

"So your dad was outnumbered, too. Is he funny?"

"My father and mother keep their heads in the clouds most of the time. Only thing I ever heard them declare amusing was a play on words in Middle English from Chaucer's *Canterbury Tales*."

Chaucer? Was Evangeline Shaw for real?

She pressed her glasses higher on her nose. "Once, my mother giggled over a scene from the Bayeux Tapestry."

"The Bayeux what?"

She fluttered her hand. "Never mind."

He stared at her.

She fidgeted. "Stop looking at me like I'm from outer space. Theirs is an acquired humor. You had to be there."

"There where?"

She sighed. "Most of their sabbaticals are spent in the French countryside. That's where they are now."

With parents like that, no wonder Evangeline Shaw loved books so much.

If anything, what he'd learned raised more questions in his mind. Like, what was someone like her—who spent vacations in France and probably spoke fluent French—doing in a tiny town in coastal Virginia? He vowed not to underestimate Miss Shaw again.

She cleared her throat. "We still haven't talked about the book yet."

"We've talked about several books."

The librarian blinked. "We did?"

"Sure, we did. The *Canterbury Tales*, *Pride and Prejudice* and that Bayeux thingy."

The librarian pushed at her glasses. "It's a tapestry, not a book."

Charlie pursed his lips. "I'll look that up when I get off duty and remedy my sadly neglected education."

Her eyes, like liquid sky, flashed. "Are you mocking me, Deputy Pruitt?"

Charlie hadn't meant to rile her. "No, ma'am. I wouldn't do that, I promise." His heart hammered.

Then, understanding dawned on her face. "This foray of yours into literature is about a woman, isn't it?" She fingered the frame of her glasses. "It has to be about a woman."

He frowned. "Why do you assume it has to be about a woman? Are *you* mocking *me* now?"

"Is it or is it not about a woman?"

He fiddled with a duck sauce packet. "In a manner of speaking, yes."

"She's the one who's the classical reader?"

This one he could answer without any check to his conscience. "She is." He opened his palms. "Out of my league entirely, but hope springs eternal."

"And this is where I and the Kiptohanock library come in?"

He gave her the tried and true, ever-reliable Charlie Pruitt grin. "Yes, ma'am."

"Okay, then. Because that's what I'm about." Her cheeks reddened. "As a librarian, I mean." She reached for the ticket.

He was a split-second quicker.

"This is supposed to be dutch treat," she protested.

"Next time you can treat me."

Her eyebrows rose almost to her hairline. "Next time?"

"There's next week's book selection. I may need more tutoring." He smiled. "By the way, what is next week's Jane Austen book club pick?"

"You're in for a treat."

He got a sinking feeling.

"Another classic, *Sense and Sensibility*." She batted those fabulous blue eyes at him. "You'll have fun explaining to the group which you like better."

Charlie slid out of the booth, the bill in his hand. "From your tone it sounds as if you're assuming I won't like *Sense and Whatever*."

She scrambled after him. "My point, I believe."

"Forget male pride. It's your own female prejudice that makes you think guys can't enjoy Jane Austen." He laughed. "Did you catch what I did there?" He stuck his thumbs into his duty belt. "Pride...and prejudice..."

The staid librarian rolled her eyes.

"And there's one other reason guys should read Jane Austen."

She reached for her purse. "What's that?"

He stuck a toothpick into the corner of his mouth. "It proves men and women can be friends."

She planted her hand on her hip. "You got that from *Pride and Prejudice*?"

He twirled the toothpick between his thumb and index finger. "I think underneath the witty banter, the reason the chemistry worked between Elizabeth and Darcy was because they valued each other as friends first and foremost."

Charlie shuffled his feet. "Maybe we can be friends, Miss Shaw."

She tilted her head. "You think because I'm new here, I don't have any friends?"

He remained silent, caught by the blond tips of her ponytail brushing across her shoulders.

She grimaced. "You wouldn't be far wrong." She extended her hand. "Call me Evy."

He reached for her hand. "Evy it is."

And she snatched the bill from him. With a triumphant glance over her shoulder, she marched toward the register. Where she proceeded to pay for both their meals while conducting a conversation with the cashier in a tongue he presumed to be Mandarin or Cantonese.

Middle English. Probably French. And now Mandarin?

Charlie held the door for her as they exited and shook his head.

Wow…not only out of his league. More like out of his galaxy.

Clapping his hat onto his head, he escorted her to the parking lot.

She dug through her purse, searching for her keys. "You don't have to wait for me."

"A Southern gentleman always waits. And it's been fun." Surprised, he realized it had been fun. With no urgent call from Dispatch, he found himself wishing dinner hadn't had to end.

Finding her key ring, she held it up for him to see. "I look forward to hearing more of your Jane Austen insights at book club."

"You and me both."

She laughed.

He scrubbed his hand over his face. "What I

meant to say was, I look forward to seeing you Thursday, too."

And he did. He'd not imagined the quiet librarian would be such good company. Or so entertaining. She was easy to be with. Despite her enormous brain, Evy Shaw wasn't pretentious.

Clicking the key fob, she unlocked her car and got inside. With a small backhanded wave, she pulled out of the parking lot and drove off into the sunset. He watched her taillights turn south on Highway 13 toward Miss Pauline's.

What was the elusive Evy Shaw after here in good ole Kiptohanock? But recon mission accomplished, he'd managed to learn enough background to call on one of his PI buddies from California who owed Charlie a favor.

His shoulder mic squawked. He responded and jogged toward his cruiser. As he headed to investigate a reported prowler, he reflected that his unofficial undercover assignment might not be so unpleasant after all.

Who'd have guessed Jane Austen could grow on a guy?

Chapter Three

Getting ready for book club on Thursday night, Evy glanced at the clock more than once. And for the fifth time, she made a minute adjustment to the way the tablecloth hung on the refreshment table. As if Charlie Pruitt would care.

The ladies—if not Charles Everett Pruitt the Third—should have been here by now. Everyone must be running late.

She plucked a pillow from the sofa in the circle of armchairs. Despite their tête-à-tête over Chinese food, she didn't think Charlie would actually show up to book club. But as she counted down the minutes, the dread—and anticipation—mounted. Her gaze flitted to the clock again.

Evy's parents had no idea what she was up to when she accepted the librarian position. Would never have envisioned their timid Evy bold enough to seek out answers to long-held questions. Would have been shocked and amazed—not to mention dismayed—at her covert attempts to learn the truth. Evy had shocked herself with her uncharacteristic behavior.

Pacing, she punched the pillow with her fist. This was so ridiculous. So high school, so—

"Hey, Evy."

She yelped and whirled. The pillow plopped onto the rug.

Arms folded across his uniformed chest, Charlie leaned against the threshold of the meeting room tucked behind the library staircase. Minus the hat for once, he grinned at her.

Her heart did a funny sort of cartwheel, so she scowled at him. She bent to retrieve the pillow at the same moment Charlie—

Their foreheads collided. She fell onto the sofa. He ricocheted into the wall.

"Ow!" She massaged her temples. "You've got a hard head, Deputy Pruitt."

"I'm not the only one." He frowned. "And I thought we'd moved past Deputy." His eyes brightened at the sight of the refreshment table. "You didn't tell me there'd be food."

He loped past Evy. "I skipped dinner for the club tonight. Can I go ahead and eat, or should I wait for the others?" His eyes scanned the room. "Where are the other ladies?"

She handed him a plate. "They're on their way with more food. Be my guest, though. Go ahead."

"How...dainty." He held a small cake square between his thumb and forefinger. "What's this? Cake for a baby?"

"Mrs. Davenport dropped those off this afternoon." Evy fanned the paper napkins on the table. "It's called a *petit four*, Charlie. It's meant to be small."

"French." He grinned. "I'm quick like that, huh?"

"You're quick like something, all right..."

Heels clicked against the hardwood floor of the library foyer.

"Yoo-hoo!" Dixie, the waitress from the Sandpiper Café, tottered into the room bearing a platter of sandwich triangles. She stuttered to a stop. "Am I interrupting something, sugar?"

Evy took a step back. She'd not realized how close she'd been standing to the deputy. "You're interrupting nothing, Dixie."

Charlie winked at Evy. "You assume Dixie was talking to *you*."

And he rested his gun-clad hip against the edge of the table. As if implying that he—as if they... Did the man never stand up straight?

She took the tray from Dixie. "Deputy Pruitt wanted to join our book club tonight."

Dixie clapped her hands together. "How fun! I had no idea the book club was going coed. Can I bring Bernie next time?"

Bernie was Dixie's husband. "Doesn't his reading tend to favor spy thrillers?"

"True. He probably wouldn't care for Jane Austen." Dixie sighed. "Because of his work with NASA at Wallop's Island, his literary tastes run toward the cloak-and-dagger stuff."

Charlie snagged a pimento cheese sandwich off the platter. "It takes a special man like *moi* to truly enjoy the classics of literature."

He helped himself to another sandwich as the other ladies arrived with additional refreshments. Evy made sure to give a special welcome to Ashley, a stay-at-home mom with three energetic children. The book club and church on Wednesday were her only nights out with grown-ups. Yet when Charlie's shoulder brushed against hers, Evy quivered.

"I caught your attempt at French, Deputy. My, my, you are quick-witted."

He pretended to tip his imaginary hat. "We deputies aim to please."

Why did Charlie Pruitt make her want to laugh?

She moved beyond him, careful not to make further contact. "Welcome, everyone."

Evy couldn't help noticing how Charlie

worked the room. He greeted every lady, who ranged in age from ninety-year-old Mrs. Evans to a thirtysomething Coastie wife. And he let them know he'd skipped supper. Evy hid her smile as she helped Reverend Parks's wife serve the punch.

The women—young and old—fell over themselves plying Charlie with food. She needn't have worried about how the ladies would receive his male intrusion into their girls' club. He was like a rooster in the proverbial henhouse. And they were loving every minute of it.

"And the petits fours?" Charlie made sure he had Evy's attention as he lifted the cake square off the plate, pinkie finger extended. "You've outdone yourself, Mrs. Davenport."

Evy almost choked on her chicken-salad sandwich. He'd mimicked the French pronunciation exactly.

"You dear boy." Mrs. Davenport fluttered her bejeweled hands like a schoolgirl. "How wonderful you know what a petit four is."

"I guess I'm just smart like that. And what they are is delicious." Charlie popped the bite-size square into his mouth.

"Let me get you another, Deputy." Mrs. Davenport, also known as the grapevine of Kiptohanock, scurried toward the table.

Charlie waggled his eyebrows at Evy. She

glared. Was the man never serious? Surely a deputy sheriff had to be more sober-minded than the likes of Charlie Pruitt.

But a smile played on her lips. He did know his way around a food table, she'd give him that. Around the ladies, too. Mr. Charming. Not her type at all. Not that Evy had a type to speak of.

At that not-so-happy thought, she took her customary armchair.

"Why don't you sit close to Evy?" Dixie hovered at Charlie's elbow. "Being a newcomer and all."

Evy's cheeks burned. She hoped no one was getting the wrong idea about her and the deputy.

"So you can see better?" Mrs. Davenport coaxed.

It wouldn't do for the ladies—or the town—to get the wrong idea. This was getting out of hand.

He slipped into a chair directly across the circle.

"No worries." Charlie leaned the chair on its back legs. "I like the view right fine from here." He sent Evy a winsome smile.

Evy peered down the length of her nose at him. "Suit yourself." She fretted at the cameo pinned to her blouse. "Shall we begin?"

Her lips might say one thing, but her heart? She didn't like what Deputy Pruitt did to her equilibrium. Not one bit.

Evy didn't have time for this…this inconvenient attraction. It went against her plan. She schooled her features. The plan must come first.

"Shall we, indeed." Charlie grinned. As if somehow he knew the effect he had on her. Raising her chin, she decided to ignore him.

He took a deep breath, which broadened his chest. As if daring her to try.

Those remarkable eyes of hers.

Charlie decided he could munch petits fours and stare at Evy Shaw all day. This club thing was turning out to be a real pleasure.

But across the circle, those eyes of hers were shooting daggers at him at this moment. Smirking, he took another bite and chewed. He loved pushing her buttons.

She reminded him of a character in the musical the drama class performed his senior year at Nandua High. In her long-sleeved peach blouse and beige pencil skirt, she looked so Marian the Librarian. So uptight and upright.

It was kind of fun to wind her up and set her off—like watching a jewelry box ballerina go all dashboard hula girl.

His mind wandered as the women discussed various themes from the novel, such as class structure and reputation. His friend in California had verified what Evy Shaw had revealed of her past.

Midtwenties. Her parents were tenured English professors from Stanford. Before she'd arrived in Kiptohanock, she'd held positions in libraries from Miami to San Diego.

He stopped chewing. While still in the Coast Guard, hadn't Sawyer Kole transferred to Kiptohanock from somewhere in California? Might prove interesting to find out where he'd been previously stationed and determine if Kole and Evy ever shared locales before Kiptohanock.

Charlie set the plate on his knee. Losing his appetite at the thought of them sharing anything, he swallowed past the boulder lodged in his throat.

Another fact he'd learned? Evy held advanced degrees in literature and library science from Stanford and the University of Oklahoma. Sawyer Kole grew up in Oklahoma.

Charlie kept his gaze laser-focused on Evy's animated features as she led the group discussion. What was her connection to Honey's husband?

Time to rattle Hula Girl again.

He cleared his throat. "One thing I found most fascinating…" the women—as if one entity—angled toward him "…was how first impressions can be deceiving."

Perched in the armchair with her brown high heels planted on the floor, Evy laid the book across her lap. "You mean how Elizabeth Bennet's first impression was that Darcy was a snob?"

Charlie rolled his tongue over his teeth. "I think that cuts both ways. Darcy and Elizabeth were both guilty of pride and prejudice."

Ashley, the wife of a former football buddy of his, nodded. "Darcy was equally guilty of prejudging Elizabeth. Based on her lack of social standing."

Charlie cocked his head. "Question is, *Miss* Shaw—are first impressions to be trusted? Or should you wait for proof that a person is trustworthy?"

She stiffened. "Sounds as if you advocate putting people on trial. Testing them before you deem them worthy of your friendship, *Deputy* Pruitt."

Their gazes locked. The librarian was hiding something. He knew it.

Kelly Hughes, the Coastie wife, brushed a crumb off her jeans. "People are not always what they seem. Each of the characters hid their real feelings behind a mask of pride."

Evy narrowed her eyes. "As a police officer, do you rely on your intuition in shaping your immediate response to people, Deputy Pruitt?"

"In cop speak, I rely on my gut. And yes, my instincts about a situation have kept me alive on more than one occasion." Charlie curled his lip. "And on a personal level, I've learned the hard way it doesn't pay to trust—or love—too blindly."

Evy's eyes bored into him. "Sounds as if someone hurt you very badly, Deputy Pruitt."

His breath hitched. An awkward silence fell. Flushing, he wasn't sure how this had become about him. Or how she'd managed to turn the discussion onto him.

Dixie patted his arm. "I think the real point of the story is how people can change."

"Given time, evaluations can alter." Mrs. Davenport wiped the corners of her mouth with a napkin. "Darcy focused on the wrong things first. But over time he saw Elizabeth for who she was. Really saw her."

Evy's brow puckered. "What do you mean?"

Peggy—his former high school math teacher who once upon a time loved marking Charlie's homework with red X's—thumbed through the pages of the novel. "He saw the real Elizabeth. And their courtship not only proved to each other their true character but also became the proving ground of their true love."

Evy ran her hand over her beige skirt. "That's very insightful."

"And—" Jolene, an ER nurse at Riverside Hospital, got up to refill her coffee cup "—it was in the crucible of crisis in their courtship that Darcy saw the error of his own ways and understood his own great love for Elizabeth."

Evy blew out a breath. "Wow. Great analysis by everyone. I've never seen the story that way before."

Mrs. Davenport tapped her finger to her chin. "It's never wise to come to a conclusion about someone until you have all the facts."

Charlie couldn't have agreed more. Which was why he'd decided to escalate his investigation. He'd never seen Evy and Kole together. Watching their interaction might provide further clues as to what was going on with a certain intriguing librarian.

Evy rose in a graceful, fluid motion. "Facts or trust? An interesting dichotomy for relationships. Which do we rely upon most often?"

Something tightened in Charlie's stomach.

Evy rubbed her finger across the rim of her glasses. "Important questions to ponder this week as we move on to next week's selection."

Her beautiful eyes sparkled. *"Sense and Sensibility."*

The meeting ended as the women cleared the refreshment table and gathered their belongings. At the ladies' teasing looks, Charlie realized he'd given the Kiptohanock matchmakers entirely the wrong impression.

And what he was about to do next would only solidify that impression. The group followed Evy out to the foyer to collect the books for the following week's discussion.

He hung back in the kitchen, waiting for Evy. "You're good with children, Evy."

She poured the remains of the coffeepot down the sink drain. "Thank you. I like children."

"That's why I hoped maybe you could help me with a project."

She rinsed out the pot. "If I can. What project?"

"It's for the department, really."

"Sheriff's business?"

"Deputy sheriff business."

Her mouth quirked. "How in the world can a librarian like me be of assistance to Super-Deputy?"

"Who?"

She bit her lip and turned to wipe the counter.

He hunched his shoulders. "The library is closed over Labor Day weekend, right?"

She unplugged the coffeemaker from the wall socket. "Yes."

"If you'd care to join me, I need to make an appearance—in an unofficial capacity—to present a friendly face behind the uniform to the kids."

Stretching on her tiptoes, she stashed the unused paper plates inside the cabinet. "What kids?"

"The kids at Keller's Kids Camp."

She froze. "Sawyer Kole's foster kid camp."

Charlie didn't like the sound of the ex-Coastie's name on her lips. "Yeah. Him."

Evy drifted onto her heels. "Isn't camp over until next summer?"

"It's a new two-month pilot program on autumn weekends. Follow-up with local foster kids. Friday night through Sunday afternoons."

She averted her gaze. "The Duers won't want me."

"With the Labor Day harbor festival and folks on their last vacation before school starts Tuesday, I have it on good authority the volunteer pool is light this weekend. Too light for the number of children expected. You'll be welcome."

She looked at him, then. As if she didn't believe him.

"We'll be doing them a favor. You'd be doing *me* a favor." He moistened his lips. "Would you come with me, Evy? Please?"

She searched his face. Not quite buying his explanation.

"I do love kids…" She gulped. "Sure. Why not? I'd love to go. Thanks for asking."

He smiled. "I'll pick you up Saturday morning. Bright and early. It's a date."

"Okay." She tucked a loosened strand of blond hair behind her ear.

Following the motion of her hand, his heart beat rapidly. Should he trust his first impressions of Evy Shaw? Sweet, smart, very pretty. Was his initial instinct about her correct?

"You don't have to wait for me, Charlie."

"Of course I do. I'll walk you to your car."

She slung the purse strap over her shoulder. "Another Southern gentleman thing?"

He followed Evy to the front door. "Let me be one, okay? And for the record, I *want* to walk you to your car."

Evy worried her bottom lip between her teeth as she set the alarm on the library. He stuffed his hands in his pockets. Before he did something stupid like touch her. Or kiss her.

Suppose he was wrong about Evy? Could she be hiding behind a mask, the image she wanted him to see? And if so, why?

Who was the real Evy Shaw? Was seeing believing in her case?

Maybe…maybe not. Only time would tell.

Chapter Four

On Saturday morning, Charlie leaned across the truck cab and threw open the passenger door. "Hop in."

The open door dinged. Evy hesitated. "Come on, Shorty."

She sniffed and placed her shoe on the running board. Putting one hand on the seat and the other on the handle, she hauled herself onto the seat. "I prefer to think of myself as vertically challenged."

He laughed and jumped out of the truck to come around and close the door for her.

"You didn't have to do that, Charlie."

He smiled. "It's going to be a great day. Buckle up. Safety first."

She smiled. "Will do, Officer." She clicked her seat belt in place.

Charlie palmed the wheel as he maneuvered

the rural road. "Glad to see you dressed appropriately."

Evy extended her feet, toes pointed. "You don't like the way I dress?"

He loved the way she dressed. The pencil skirts, high heels and silky blouses. But his favorite was the baby-blue cardigan she'd worn to the Chinese restaurant, which brought out the blue in her eyes. Charlie scrubbed a hand over his face. Since when did he have favorites where Evy Shaw was concerned?

Charlie stole a quick look at her. He liked her version of casual, too. The pink polka-dot Keds. The lime-green boatneck T-shirt. The cuffed jeans.

Only her ponytail retained her usual weekday appearance. And idly he wondered what her hair would look like spilling over her shoulders... gleaming in the sunshine...

His heartbeat staccato-stepped. "I like the way you dress just fine."

Evy's eyebrows rose as his voice went gravelly. He'd surprised her. Surprised him, too. Who would have guessed, in casual Kiptohanock, he'd take a shine to someone like Evy Shaw?

A shine... He lifted his ball cap off his head and resettled it. Where did that come from?

Sounded like something Charlie's grandfather

would've said fifty years ago. Evy had a way of bringing out the old-fashioned in him. She smiled at Charlie. And his heart flip-flopped inside his chest.

With effort, he refocused on the road. Was she happy to be riding in a truck with him? Or happy at the prospect of spending the day with the Duers? And if so, why?

Doubt ate at his stomach. He hadn't always been so unsure of himself. But his confidence where women were concerned had taken a nosedive since his days with Honey.

He pulled into the long gravel driveway of the Keller farmhouse. Passing under the crossbars framing the entrance to the farm, the truck rattled over a cattle guard. Cedars and fencing lined the drive. Horses grazed in the pasture.

She sat forward on the seat. Her gaze flitted from side to side. Taking everything in. "I've never been here before."

"Me neither."

Her eyes darted to him. "You didn't volunteer over the summer?"

"Nope. My first time to help out, too."

"Oh."

He'd have given a week's salary to know what was going through that brilliant mind of hers. He didn't have to wait long.

"Why not?"

He rapped his thumb against the steering wheel. "Too busy."

"Too busy doing deputy stuff?"

"Something like that."

He steered the truck beside a bevy of other vehicles outside the hip-roofed barn. "We're here." Parking, he allowed the swirl of dust heralding their arrival to settle.

Charlie spotted Sawyer Kole in the corral with a handful of children and a horse. The very pregnant Honey rested against the fence railing. Charlie was nervous. Nervous about what would happen next.

About how Honey would react to Evy being here. About how Sawyer would respond to *him* being here. Sure enough, when Charlie unfolded himself out of the truck, Sawyer's arctic-blue eyes narrowed. Evy opened her door and got out.

Following her husband's belligerent stare, Honey turned. "Charlie? What are—?"

Charlie knew the moment Evy stepped around the truck.

Because Honey went ramrod stiff. "What's *she* doing here?"

Her husband refastened his gaze onto Evy. Sawyer took a step forward. Frowned. Halted in his tracks. The lead on the horse hung limply in his hand.

Charlie's heart pounded. He didn't like the intense look Sawyer gave Evy. Did they know each other?

Evy inched closer to Charlie. At his elbow, she shrunk into his side. Doing that melding thing she did. For protection? For invisibility?

Broadening his shoulders, Charlie creased the brim of his cap with his hand. "We came to volunteer. Heard you might need a few more hands with so many folks away for Labor Day weekend."

Sawyer seemed to come to himself. "Don't believe I've had the pleasure of meeting your friend." He looped the lead around a fence post and came out of the corral. Wiping his palm on the side of his Wrangler jeans, Sawyer headed their way, hand extended to Evy. "I'm Sawyer."

Charlie's gaze bounced between Evy and Kole.

Behind the glasses, those enormous eyes of hers had fixed onto the cowboy. And she moved away from Charlie to grasp hold of Sawyer's hand.

Charlie's stomach cramped. Something curled in his chest. Suddenly he wanted nothing more than to pick Evy up in his arms, plop her inside his truck and speed away.

Toward hot cups of tea, Chinese food and library books. He shouldn't have brought her here. She—he—they didn't belong here.

She's mine, he wanted to shout. *Not yours.*

But he did none of that. Like an idiot, Charlie just stood there. Hands stuffed into his jeans pockets. Watching. While Sawyer Kole inexplicably took someone else from him.

"My name is Evy." A shy smile, which twisted Charlie's gut. "Evy Shaw."

Sawyer's brow knotted. "How is it, in a town the size of Kiptohanock, we haven't met before, Miss Shaw?"

Charlie's heart thumped in his chest. Honey followed on her husband's boot heels. With one look at her face, Charlie could tell Honey was furious. At him.

"She's the librarian." Honey glowered. "No reason for you to have met."

Charlie had wanted Sawyer and Evy to meet officially. He ought to have been more careful what he wished for. Sucker-punched by the unexpected sense of proprietorship toward Evy, he ground his heel into the dirt. She didn't belong to him. He didn't know why seeing her and Sawyer together disturbed him so much. Honey was right about it not being a romantic kind of connection. But there was a connection, something Charlie didn't understand.

So he drew on his fallback emotion when it came to feeling out of control. Anger.

He inserted himself between the cowboy and Evy. "I guess not everyone is a reader like me."

Evy's gaze flicked to Charlie. "No." A sweet smile for him. "That's true."

"I feel somehow, though, we've met before." Sawyer tilted his head. "Do we know each other, Miss Shaw? From somewhere besides Kiptohanock?"

Charlie held his breath. Evy—with reluctance, he thought—shook her head. Disappointment spiraled. He let the breath trickle slowly between his clenched lips.

So this was about Evy. All about her. Not Kole. Which only made Charlie feel worse, not better. Honey had been right about Evy's fixation on the Duer clan. Did Evy have a sinister motivation in coming to the Shore?

"Put us to work, Kole. That's what we're here for." His mouth tightened. "Don't look a gift horse in the mouth."

The look Sawyer sent his way could have scorched the earth. "That your way of talking so somebody like me can understand?" There'd never been any love lost between him and Charlie.

Honey gripped Sawyer's sleeve. "Sawyer..."

"If the horseshoe fits." Charlie jutted his jaw. "Then, yeah."

He and Kole were never destined to be friends. Too much history. Bad history.

Sawyer pushed the brim of the Stetson higher onto his forehead.

Charlie frowned. Sawyer's gesture seemed familiar. But he couldn't place where or why.

"Maybe you and Miss Shaw could help Mr. Keller with the other group of kids by the creek." The smile Sawyer threw his way wasn't meant to be friendly. "And leave the cowboying to the real cowboys, Deputy." His attention returning to Evy, Sawyer tipped his hat. "Ma'am."

Charlie's blood boiled. Cupping her elbow in his palm, he gritted his teeth and dragged Evy around the corner of the house.

He didn't like the way Evy peered over her shoulder, focusing on Honey and Sawyer as they walked away. She stumbled.

"Watch where you're going, *Miss Shaw*," he growled.

Evy stopped. "Are you mad about something?" she whispered. "Mad at me?" She blinked rapidly behind the glass frames.

Charlie hated the uncertainty in her voice. And one look at those eyes of hers... He had no right to be angry at her.

No business taking out his angst about Sawyer Kole—Honey, too, if the whole truth were told—on Evy.

He let go of her. "Is there a reason I should be mad at you, Evy? You haven't done anything wrong, have you?"

The bridge between her perfectly arched brows pinched. "No, I guess not." Biting her lip, her eyes skittered over the silver ribbon of the tidal creek.

She was lying. Or at best, hiding something.

Abruptly he veered toward the creek bank, where a cluster of children surrounded old Mr. Keller and a thirtysomething woman Charlie didn't recognize. He left Evy to follow. Or not.

"Reinforcements. Hoorah." Mr. Keller raised a child-sized fishing rod. "I was wondering how Felicia and I were going to drive the boat, bait hooks and make sure no one drowns."

The lady helped a child thread his arms into a life preserver. "I'm Felicia Kerr. I'm a counselor with the county here to help the children get reacquainted with their siblings."

"Charlie Pruitt."

Mr. Keller handed around more life jackets. "Charlie is a deputy sheriff, kids."

One or two of the children went motionless. Charlie understood. Some of these children's only experience with a deputy had been the day when they'd been forcibly removed from their families for various reasons. He hoped by getting to know him, the children would gain more positive impressions of law enforcement.

Evy ventured onto the small dock. "I'm Evy Shaw."

Charlie did his best to ignore the feelings—like dragonfly wings frolicking against his skin—her proximity evoked. He reached for the bait bucket. "We're here to serve. Put us to work."

Mr. Keller pointed his chin at Evy. "You're the new librarian, aren't you?"

"Guilty as charged. I'm afraid I'm not very water-savvy." She wrinkled her nose at the fishy smell emanating from the bucket. "Or experienced in fishing. Are we going to have to touch those things?"

The children surged toward Charlie and peered at the contents of the bucket. "Oooh... gross...cool..."

A mocha-skinned little girl with colorful barrettes in the cornrows of her hair hung back. "I can't get the buckle to click."

Evy went down on one knee to inspect the orange life vest. "Let me see what I can do." She untangled the clasp and clicked it closed. "There. What's your name?"

"Latasha." Her large brown eyes grew fearful. "I've never been on a boat before. S'pose I fall out?"

Evy took the child's hand. "You hang on to me, and I'll hang on to you. We'll make sure neither one of us falls out, okay?"

Latasha hugged Evy's hand. "Do you know how to swim?"

"Actually, not so well." Evy gestured at Charlie. "But see this big guy here?"

Latasha gave Charlie a quick up-and-down appraisal.

"He knows how to rescue people." Evy aimed her mouth in the direction of his ear. "You do know how to rescue people, don't you?"

Charlie crouched beside Latasha. "I worked as a lifeguard at the pool when I was in high school."

Evy smirked. "Of course you did."

"Come on, Latasha," called a boy, already seated in the boat.

"That's my brother." Latasha twined her fingers into Evy's. "We don't live together anymore."

"You must miss him." Evy stared at the water, glittering like diamonds in the early morning sun. "I sure would."

Charlie stared at her. Something fretted at the edges of his consciousness.

She dropped her gaze. "I mean, if I had a brother."

Latasha poked out her lips. "I miss my brother a lot."

Evy's eyes welled. "How wonderful it is, though, that you get to spend the weekend together at camp."

Charlie reached for Evy's other hand. "I think you'll like fishing, Latasha, if you give it a chance. It's pretty out on the water and peaceful waiting for the fish to bite."

"Okay... I'll try if you will, Evy."

She didn't let go of Evy's hand as they stepped aboard Keller's boat. The next few minutes were spent making sure everyone applied sunscreen.

As the boat chugged away from the dock, Keller pointed out the string of barrier islands across the tidal marsh, which emptied into the Atlantic. He increased the throttle as they left the shore behind. "I know a great little fishing hole, kids," Keller shouted above the roar of the motor.

With the children laughing at the antics of shorebirds swooping in lazy figure eights over their heads in the bright September sky, Charlie propped his elbows against the railing. His favorite type of day. Out on the water.

He glanced over at Latasha perched in Evy's lap. "Not so bad, see?"

The wind whipped through Evy's hair and loosened her ponytail. She brushed a strand out of her eyes only to have it fly into her face again as the boat gained speed. She grimaced. He laughed and gave in to the urge to touch her hair.

He caught the silky blond lock between his thumb and forefinger. He tucked the tendril behind her ear, and his hand lingered. The bottom dropped out of his stomach. Looking into her eyes, he felt weightless.

Flushing, Charlie dropped his hand. And found Keller's gaze on him. Keller winked.

The children squealed with excitement as the boat skimmed over the blue-green waves of the Machipongo Inlet. Evy did not. By the time Keller dropped anchor, she appeared a bit green herself.

Charlie, Keller and Felicia got busy showing the children how to bait their hooks. Latasha hopped off Evy's lap and entered into the joy of the day. At first, Evy moved from one child to the next. Offering her encouragement, if not her expertise.

But finally she sank onto the seat at the railing. Her mouth thinned. A sheen of sweat broke out on her lip.

Charlie headed over to her. "Are you okay, Evy?"

She gave him a wobbly smile. "I—I don't feel so good."

"Try not to stare at the horizon. It's the motion of the boat on the waves. It distorts your perspective and unsettles your equilibrium."

She squeezed her eyes closed. She clutched her stomach.

"Mr. Deputy?"

He left Evy for a moment to help one youngster untangle his line.

Planting their feet even with their hips to widen their center of gravity, the children stood shoulder to shoulder around the perimeter of the boat. They called to each other, teasing each other, as the water tugged on their lines.

Latasha elbowed him. "Evy don't look so good, Mr. Deputy."

He pivoted. No, she didn't. Then Evy leaned over the side of the boat and vomited.

He hurried over to her. "Evy?"

She retched again and again. He kept his hand on her shoulder. Silent tears rolling down her face, she emptied her stomach until dry heaves remained.

"I'm so sorry." Embarrassment flushed her cheeks. "I'm so sorry."

He ran his hand over the crown of her head. "It's okay, Evy."

"No," her lips trembled. "It's not."

Felicia fished a tissue out of her jeans and gave it to Evy.

He extracted a bottle of water from the cooler. He unscrewed the cap. "Swish out your mouth and spit it over the side."

Latasha left her fishing pole. "It's okay, Evy," She patted Evy's back. "I'll take care of you." She sounded like a little mother.

Evy's arm went around the child's waist. "I'm supposed to be taking care of you, Latasha. Not the other way around."

Latasha smiled. "We'll take care of each other."

"Sorry to be such a landlubber," Evy whispered to him.

"It's okay. Really. Most of us on the Shore have been out on the water since we could walk. You'll get used to it."

Evy's eyes clouded. The supercompetent librarian didn't like feeling inadequate.

"Once we get underway back to shore, it won't be so bad."

"I don't want to cut short the children's fun."

Mr. Keller shook his head. "These small fry have been baking in the sun long enough. Time to get back for lunch."

At his words, Evy moaned.

Charlie eased onto the seat beside her. "Did you eat anything this morning before we left?"

She shook her head.

"An empty stomach is the worst on the water."

Evy looked at him as if she didn't believe it.

"No, truly. Once you eat something, you'll feel—"

She groaned. "I may never eat again."

"Crackers. Baby steps before you decide to starve yourself forever."

"Fine." She put a hand to her head. "But can we stop talking about food?"

"Whatever you say."

Evy's mouth curved up. "I reserve the right to remind you of that later."

He laughed. "Good to know you haven't lost your sense of humor."

She made a face. "Just my appetite and my pride."

Evy held on to Charlie's arm for support as they stepped onto dry land. Weaving, unsteady on her feet. If only the ground would stop moving.

"I suppose you'd think me melodramatic if I dropped and kissed the ground." She hung her head. "If I can find it."

"Your equilibrium will stabilize in a few minutes, I promise. Take some deep breaths."

But she was mortified. Could she appear any more inadequate? She had to vomit in front of

Charlie, of all the people in the world. Still, hanging on to his arm wasn't the worst way she'd ever spent a morning.

The scent she was coming to associate with Charlie Pruitt—clean soap and cinnamon gum—floated across her personal space.

Charlie Pruitt was a nice guy. A true Virginia gentleman. Sort of old-fashioned. Her favorite kind of hero.

She might not have as much experience as most women, but she had enough to know that nice guys like him weren't a dime a dozen.

Charlie stiffened at the sight of Honey Kole, arms crossed, at the top of the slope. "Why don't you go help Wanda and Betty set out the box lunches for the children, Evy?"

"Where will you be?"

His gaze cut to Honey. "I'll be along in a minute. Don't worry about me."

Feeling abandoned—not a new sensation—Evy drew herself up and plodded toward the screened porch where two ladies from church poured water into plastic cups. She reached for the handle of the screen door when—

"Why did you bring her here, Charlie?" Honey hissed. "You're going to ruin everything."

Over her shoulder, Evy watched him hustle Honey around the corner of the house, out of earshot. Something was going on between them. Unfinished business?

Evy was surprised by the fierce possessiveness she felt toward Charlie. Swinging open the door to the creak of hinges, she reminded herself that Charlie's past relationships weren't her concern.

After lunch, she accompanied Latasha's group to the corral. Charlie, Felicia and Mr. Keller departed with the other group in the boat. Evy's stomach had settled, thanks to the crackers Charlie had scrounged up for her. Under Honey's scornful eye. Too late, Evy figured, to fly under the radar with her.

She was beginning to understand how Alice felt falling through the proverbial rabbit hole. Evy resisted an inward shudder. The Duer sisters were intimidating to someone like her. Especially Honey, Delmarva's Hostess with the Mostest and owner of the Duer Lodge. Because Evy wasn't the Mostest at anything. Except at keeping secrets.

Individually, the women made Evy anxious. Collectively, she became mute in their presence.

But Sawyer's pregnant wife, Honey—with the sweet smile and Southern belle pearls—terrified Evy. Somehow people know when they're not liked. And the Duers—mostly Honey—didn't like Evy.

Evy wasn't sure what had given her away. She was usually forgettable and easily overlooked. But she'd been shut out of the Fourth of July planning committee, headed by Honey. And Evy's offer to volunteer at Keller's Kids Camp for foster siblings this summer had been ignored until Charlie brought her here today.

Nor was she sure what her end goal had been in her thwarted attempts to infiltrate the Duer clan. Reconciliation, a long shot. If nothing else, a long overdue closure.

She was nervous enough without Honey's watchful glare. Like she was just waiting for Evy to make a fool out of herself. Evy had been scared to death meeting Sawyer that morning. Scared and excited all at the same time. Finally, the chance to get to know her long-lost brother.

And when he didn't recognize her? Relief followed by a sharp disappointment. But it was for the best, she rationalized. Their lives were so different. They hadn't seen each other since they were children, when Evy had been adopted out of their foster home.

Leaning against the gate, she watched as he gave instructions to the children on how to mount a horse and how to tuck their sneakers into the stirrups. She was the ultimate non-out-doorsy girl. He was so in his element.

One by one, Sawyer led the children around

the corral. "Nice and easy. Sit back in the saddle. Hold the reins loose in your hands," he said to them.

Several children refused to get close to the horses, however, much less ride. Including Latasha.

The little girl remained glued to Evy's side, watching, like Evy, from a distance. "They look ginormous," Latasha whispered.

Evy patted her. "Sawyer said there's nothing to be afraid of. That the horses are very gentle and used to kids."

Latasha poked out her lip. "Then how come you're not riding?"

Good point. Somehow Evy had to find a way to harness her own terror. The children climbed onto the railing. Why couldn't she be braver?

Holding on to the bridle, Sawyer led the horse over to them. "Sure you don't want to join us, Miss Shaw?"

The horse nibbled at Evy through the railing. She shied away as drool dribbled on her hand.

"I—I don't think so." She gave a self-deprecating laugh. "I always wanted to learn how to ride, but my parents didn't think it was a good idea." She laced her fingers together. "Me, the preteen girl who devoured every horse book in the library. Silly, huh?" She shrugged.

"Not silly, Miss Shaw. They're wonderful

companions. Loyal. Hardworking. Magnificent."

"I just never imagined them to be so—"

"So big?"

Evy glanced into Sawyer's light blue eyes and found sympathy. "I'm not a very good example to the children. Nor have I made much of a contribution today." She surveyed the farm. "This is way outside my comfort zone."

"It's okay to be scared. Everybody gets scared when it's something they've never done before."

He smiled, the corner of his mouth lifting. "I hear you're very smart. We make contributions by using the skills that God has gifted us with. Maybe not fishing or horses. But I'm sure we can find a place for you at Keller's Kids Camp. The children like you. And in my book—" he smiled "—no pun intended to librarians, their trust in you is worth more than anything else."

She relaxed a smidgeon. Sawyer Kole was one of the nicest men she'd ever met, she decided. Other than Charlie. Honey was a lucky woman. Evy hoped she knew that.

"Maybe some other time when there's less commotion, you could give it a try."

She so wanted Sawyer's approval. "Maybe…"

Tipping his hat to her, he led the horse back to the barn. Several ladies motioned the kids toward tables underneath the leafy canopy of the pecan trees. Craft time, judging from the construction paper, glue and assorted markers strewn across the tables.

Hearing footsteps, Evy turned as Felicia approached.

The brunette smiled. "Just the person I was looking for."

Evy let out a sigh. "Then you might be the only one."

"You're the town librarian, right?"

She nodded.

"Many of these children—" Felicia's brown eyes flicked around the farmyard "—have suffered trauma at the hands of those who were supposed to love them the most. Separated from everyone and everything they knew, most of them have learned to hide their true feelings behind masks."

"All they had was each other." Evy felt as if a heavy weight pressed on her chest. Making it hard to breathe. "Then they were ripped away from brothers and sisters."

"Exactly." Felicia cocked her head. "I think you might be the perfect person to help me."

"Help you?" Evy frowned. "I don't understand."

"I outlined my plan to Mr. Keller on our last boat trip. He thought it was a great idea. I'm sure the Koles will agree. Something right up your alley."

Evy had her doubts Honey Kole would agree with anything that involved her. "What plan?"

"I heard about the children's story time you do at the library. I wonder if we could do the same thing this weekend with selected picture books to help the children open up about their feelings and process what has happened to them."

Felicia gave a thumbs-up to a child calling her name who held up a drawing for the counselor to admire. "After summer camp was so successful, we decided to try this pilot program for local foster children. The same children will come back to the farm every weekend. Would you be willing to commit your Saturday evenings for the rest of the program?"

A slow ember of excitement grew within Evy. Read a book? Was Felicia kidding? That was something Evy could certainly do. "Each night before lights-out?"

Felicia smiled. "You'd take lead on reading the story in the girls' cabin. And maybe we could talk Deputy Pruitt into leading story time in the boys' cabin since he's such a reader."

Evy laughed.

Felicia gave her a quizzical smile. "You don't think it's a good idea?"

"I think it's a wonderful idea." Evy caught

sight of Charlie headed toward them. "Charlie *is* a great reader. I'm sure he'll love it."

"Good. I have a list of recommended books. Do you know if the library carries these?" Felicia unfolded the paper she removed from her shirt pocket. "Sorry for the squiggly lines. As you know, the boat doesn't stay still while you try to write."

Evy scanned the items. "Our collection contains four of the six. I'll check them out this afternoon."

Felicia clapped her hands. "Thank you so much. Will you explain the plan to Deputy Pruitt? You don't think he'll mind?"

Evy tucked the paper inside her back pocket. "I'm sure he won't mind. He'll love adding another book to his to-be-read pile."

Chapter Five

Later that evening, Charlie gaped at Evy. "You want me to do what?"

"I guess I should've checked with you first. I forgot about you having to go back to work."

He fidgeted. "I don't have another tour until Labor Day, actually."

"I thought this would be something for me to do to help these children. To make a difference in a small way." She fiddled with the bread stick. "I'm sorry."

"Quit saying that." He sighed. "And I'm sorry. I didn't think about you not liking Italian."

"I like Italian. See?" She bit off a chunk of the bread and chewed. "You're a great cook. I'm just excited."

Charlie could tell she was excited. After craft time, he and Evy left Keller's to retrieve the library books. And grab a bite to eat.

He'd had about all the camp food he could stomach for one day. He liked little kids a bunch. He liked grown-up time with Evy Shaw even more.

So he'd gone out on a limb and invited Evy over to his house for lasagna. He liked seeing her here. She looked good in his kitchen. At his table.

"I may not be able to swing it every weekend. Depends on the schedule."

"Of course. Maybe someone else could take your place on the nights you're not able to come."

Which sent a shaft into his heart. "That's me." He tried to play it off. "Easily replaced."

She placed her hands on either side of her plate. "That's not what I meant. You're not easily replaced. Not to me."

Evy fingered the gold-rimmed edge of the dinner plate. His grandmother's Sunday china. Yeah, he'd gone all out.

"Is that how you feel?" Evy frowned. "Is that what you think happened between you and Honey?"

He jerked. "How do you—what have you heard?"

"Nothing, but I can see how you look at her when you think no one is looking. Honey's the one who hurt you, isn't she, Charlie?"

He scraped back his chair. "Who's been talking behind my back?"

"Just my initial impression watching the tension between you two today." She caught his arm as he reached for her plate. "I'm a good listener if you want to talk about it. Friends, remember?"

Friends? He wrenched free of her hold on his arm and lifted the plate. She knotted her fingers into her lap.

"Trust me, whatever happened or didn't happen with Honey is in the past. Where it belongs."

She shook her head. "Sometimes the past refuses to stay buried. But it can't remain there if that's what it takes for us to move forward."

He moved toward the kitchen. "To something better? Speak for yourself. You're not exactly the poster child for spilling your guts about your own past."

She pushed back her chair and followed him. "What did your intuition tell you about me, Deputy Pruitt? Am I to be trusted or not?"

He set the plates down. "My gut tells me you are a nice lady who loves children and books."

"I'm a librarian. So much for your superior detecting skills." She tilted her head. "Was that all you got from your first impression?"

"First impressions, as in P and P, evolve. Like trust. Time will tell."

She propped, chin in hand, on the counter. "P and P? Sounds like a sandwich. Or a grocery store. But I'm glad to know that literature is having such a profound impact on your life. Can I ask you a personal question?"

He blinked at the sudden change in topic. Why did he sense land mines ahead? He blew out a breath. "Sure. Go ahead."

"Is Honey the reason why you don't like Sawyer Kole?"

What Charlie didn't like was how those big blue eyes of Evy's followed Kole's every move. Charlie knew he was being ridiculous. And pathetic.

But with those megawatt eyes turned on him right now, he had a hard time concentrating, much less remembering why exactly he didn't like Kole. Oh, yeah. Honey.

The love of his life? He was beginning to wonder. Maybe not so much.

"Who's the real Charlie Pruitt?" He shrugged. "Raised in a house full of boys. One sister. And yes, I live in the same house I grew up in. No mystery here. I'm an open book."

Unlike Evy Shaw.

He lifted his shoulders and let them drop. "What you see is what you get. How about you?"

He'd avoided her real question. Not so much an open book. But Evy had no right to expect total disclosure if she was unwilling to offer it herself.

She glanced around the cozy interior of the two-story Victorian. The kitchen had been modernized, but the rest of the house reflected its nineteenth-century charm. "This feels like a real home."

After rinsing off the plates, Charlie turned off the faucet. "It was my grandmother's house. My dad grew up here. Now I live here."

He looked at Evy. And waited. Waited for her to share.

She took a breath. "My parents were into sleek, avant-garde modern decor. Lots of bookshelves, though."

He smirked. "Why doesn't that surprise me?"

She wandered over to the bay window in the living room and moved aside the curtain. From there, she could see beyond the corner to the gazebo on the square and the outline of the library. Maples and oaks canopied the street. "The trees will be beautiful in a few weeks."

He came alongside her. "Red and yellow. And the oak in the backyard is the most vivid orange I've ever seen in my life. You've got to see it to believe it."

If she'd had any sense at all, she would have left Kiptohanock. Mission accomplished, nothing but potential heartache awaited if she remained. She'd found her brother.

But instead of closure, Evy had discovered only more unanswered questions. Mainly about herself. And a certain deputy sheriff. Not what she'd come to Kiptohanock looking for. Yet here she was.

She contemplated the front room with its comfortable chintz sofas and well-cared-for antiques scattered among more practical pieces of modern living. Like the flat-screen mounted above the mantel over the wood-burning fireplace. A lived-in home. "It's not like the museum I grew up in." She smiled. "I'd love a tour if we have time before we head back to Mr. Keller's."

"If not, I can always put the siren on."

"Really?" Her eyes widened. "You can do that? That would be fun."

"I was kidding. That would be against regulations unless we were on official business."

"Oh." She pushed the bridge of her glasses farther up her nose.

He looked at her funny. She dropped her hand. It was a nervous habit to touch her glasses for reassurance.

"But once we get out of town, then we can let it rip."

"Fabulous…"

Charlie smiled. "If that's all it takes to please you, Evy Shaw, then you're one in a million."

He steered her into the foyer with its beautiful oak door and glass-paned sidelights. Up the ornately carved staircase to the landing's oval stained-glass window.

"I love it. So old-fashioned."

He loped down the stairs two steps at a time and waited for her at the bottom. "One more room. A special surprise I saved for last."

Coming down more slowly, Evy had a sudden flash of a long white dress trailing on the carpet runner behind her. And of herself pausing by the Tiffany-inspired window on the landing. Gazing below to where Charlie stood now, one hand propped on the newel post, waiting with her friends and family—

Snap out of it, Evy.

Evy tamped down the silly, romantic illusions. She was a librarian, not a Jane Austen heroine. Best to keep her feet and her dreams planted firmly on the ground.

After all, she'd met Charlie only because he was trying to impress a girl. She sighed. Story of her life.

Surrounded by her beloved books at the library was akin to being enveloped in the warm embrace of friends. A home away from home.

Between the pages of books, she'd found beloved childhood companions. Like Anne and Gilbert. Tom and Huckleberry Finn. And later, during her socially awkward teen years, she'd discovered Mr. Darcy and Elizabeth, Emma and Mr. Knightley.

Who was she kidding? She was still socially awkward. It hadn't taken Evy long to understand real life wasn't like books. Or real love, either. She never knew what to say to boys, nor they to her. Romance wasn't something she envisioned in her future.

It was far safer to cling to her beautiful world of books. Safe until the moment she set foot in coastal Kiptohanock.

When she reached the bottom of the staircase, he crossed the hall to a door opposite the front parlor. "You're going to love this room."

Opening the door with a flourish, he ushered her inside. With a flick of the light switch, the room blazed to life.

She took two steps inside the pine-paneled room, stopped and did a slow three-sixty. "A library? You have a library? In your house?"

Her mouth fell open at the sight of a window nook overlooking the front street.

"Dad called it the study."

Charlie leaned against the doorjamb, feet crossed at the ankle. Pleased with himself. "I thought you'd get a kick out of the window seat.

My sister's favorite place to curl up with a book when she was little. You'd like Anna."

"It's…it's…" Evy clasped her hands under her chin. "Wonderful."

He laughed. "Book heaven, huh?"

Unable to help herself, she plopped onto the plump cushions of the window seat and drew her legs up under her. Floor-to-ceiling bookshelves bracketed the wall. Masculine leather sofas dotted the room.

"My grandmother was a big reader. Dad, too. Though he's more of a Zane Grey/Louis L'Amour kind of guy. It's not for lack of trying on my mom's part that I'm a nonreader. She read to us every night when we were little."

Evy closed her eyes. Perfection. She could just imagine cuddling here with a small child while reading a storybook. Her eyes flew open. She gestured toward Charlie's copy of *Sense and Sensibility* lying on the coffee table between the sofa and armchairs. "What do you mean you're a nonreader?"

"I'm a work in progress."

She swung her legs to the floor. "Is it working? Impressing that girl?"

His brow puckered. "Who?" The line in his forehead eased. "Oh. Her." He looked away. "That's a work in progress, too."

She grabbed one of the pillows and held it

against her stomach. "Have I run across this lucky lady yet?" Evy fretted the corded fringe on the pillow. "Never mind." She fluttered her hand. "None of my business."

He wouldn't meet her eyes. Glancing everywhere but at Evy. "Sort of."

Who was it? Not that it mattered if he was hung up on some other girl. He seemed the type who was as solid and steadfast as the earth.

She tucked her tongue inside her cheek. Impressions could be deceiving. What did she really know about Charlie? What did she really know about anyone other than the person they chose to present to the world?

"What made you go into law enforcement, Charlie?"

Perching on the armrest of the sofa, he snapped his gaze to hers. "My dad retired from the Accomack County Sheriff's Department. Hokey, but I always wanted to be just like him. He taught us to care about our community. To believe in truth and justice. To want to protect those who can't protect themselves."

Evy's instincts told her to trust Charlie. He was funny and sweet and—*but don't forget*—bitter about Honey.

His reputation as a Pruitt and as a member of the law-enforcement community were very important to Charlie. They were his entire identity.

Were Evy's initial instincts wrong about him? Was he using her only as a means to an end? Was she being stupid and naive?

Perhaps this wasn't the right time to leave Kiptohanock. Maybe her mission wasn't as complete as she'd believed. Not with Sawyer's happiness at stake.

Her heartbeat quickened. Or was that merely an excuse to justify staying in town with Charlie a little while longer?

Chapter Six

That night, story time at Keller's Kids Camp went surprisingly well. In the boys' cabin, Charlie read a copy of the same story Evy read to the girls. A touching story about how it was okay to miss someone and what to do while waiting to be reunited.

Afterward she was strangely quiet. Quiet even for a librarian. Ill at ease.

Despite her prim-and-proper demeanor, Evy had always been so talkative with him. And the change from their friendly banter to awkward silence bothered Charlie. More than he liked to admit.

Had he somehow hurt her feelings? Done something to offend her? He'd lain awake half the night, reconstructing every conversation.

She'd seemed to enjoy dinner. But sometime

after their heart-to-heart, she left him. Emotionally, if not physically.

Maybe telling him about her family put her on edge. It hurt him to think of her alone except for the attention of a paid housekeeper. Anxious, afraid. Or was he projecting his own insecurities on her? Because after what happened with Honey, he understood about feeling insecure.

The next day, as the organ pounded out the opening hymn, he watched her enter the church. And aim for being unobtrusive as she slipped into one of the back pews. As if she earned the right to belong only by making herself as invisible as possible. As if she, being herself, was somehow less than.

Snagging a bulletin, he pondered if that was how she'd survived and endured what sounded to him like a lonely childhood. Totally different from his carefree Eastern Shore experience.

Charlie wove his way through the stragglers trying to find a seat as the service began in earnest. Nobody, especially someone as wonderful as Evy, got ignored. Not on his watch.

He slid into the pew next to her. Her eyes, as soft and brilliant as a blue jay's wings, glanced at him. And once again, he felt his stomach drop, weightless, as if he'd risen too fast in an elevator.

"This seat taken?"

She shook her head. But by the slight lift in her lips, he knew she was glad to see him. And pleasing her pleased him.

At the final hymn, her eyes became luminous. Something about a balm in Gilead that soothed wounded souls. The last chords of the postlude echoed in the rafters in the century-old church. People exited the pews to greet friends and neighbors. She remained motionless, a serene expression on her face.

"I never knew it could be like this." Her eyes fixed on the stained-glass depiction of Jesus on the baptistry wall. "Peaceful. Hopeful. Joyful."

"Your family aren't churchgoers?"

A small, timid smile. "Christmas. Easter. A concert or two. But not every church is like this." She gazed at the milling crowd. "From time to time, I've sensed what you have here in other places." Evy steepled her hands in her lap. "During evensong at a cathedral in the south of France. In a quiet, country church down a hedgerow lane in the middle of Somerset, England." She looked at him. "You're blessed to have grown up here in this place with these people."

He'd never looked at it that way before. But he supposed, deep in his heart, he knew that already. Maybe that was why, unlike his siblings who'd left the Eastern Shore, he'd been content

to remain. Even when, after the public humili-
ation over Honey, it would've been easier to go
off-Shore.

Evy smoothed her hand over her dress. "I
learn something new every time I come inside
these walls."

Charlie learned something new about Evy
Shaw every time he was with her. And it was
shaping up to be quite a journey of discovery.

Honey brushed by, throwing a heated glare
in their direction. Evy bit her lip as Sawyer's
shadow fell over them. Charlie's gut tightened.

"Miss Shaw."

Evy smiled at the Coastie cowboy, dropkick-
ing Charlie's pride.

Sawyer's eyes glinted. "Pruitt."

"Kole," Charlie grunted. And was glad when
the former puddle pirate moved on.

When Honey's sisters ambled past, Charlie
felt Evy shrink. He frowned. Why was she so
scared of the Duers? What power did they hold
to cause Evy such fear?

He felt their speculative glances as they
towed their hungry children toward the door.
Evy wilted with relief as the door closed behind them.

Charlie laid his arm across the back of the
pew, close but not touching her. "Speaking of
hungry…"

"Were we? Speaking of hunger?"

"I'm always thinking, if not speaking, about food." He cocked his head. "Do you know me at all?"

"Not as well as I'd like." And then her eyes bugged out behind her glass rims.

He laughed. "How about—"

Evy's lips twitched.

He edged closer. "You find it funny how I— how we—talk around here?" The swaying tips of her ponytail brushed his arm.

"I find the Tidewater brogue sweet and charming."

He rolled his eyes. "News flash. Sweet and charming is *not* the effect most guys go for."

She smiled at him over the top of her glasses. "How *aboot* what?"

"Now you're just mocking me." He feigned sliding out of the pew. "If you're going to make fun of me, you've talked yourself out—"

She pursed her lips and mouthed *oot*.

He crossed his arms over his chest. "Keep it up, sweetheart, and you'll miss the best fried chicken and french fries on the Shore. You Californians eat fried chicken, don't you?"

"Sweet tea, too. *Y'all* made a believer out of me." She nudged him. "You caught that fitting-in-with-the-locals thing I just did, right?"

He grinned. This was the Evy he'd come to know. And love?

That wiped the smile off his face. "You're as funny as a heart attack, Evy Shaw."

"Is that what the chicken is going to do to my arteries?"

He wagged his finger in her face. "Just for that, I'm not going to order you a milk shake."

Gripping the pew in front of them, she rose and scooted past him. "That'll teach me."

"So, is it a date or what?" He scrambled into the aisle. "Can we take your car? I walked to church from the house."

On the steps of the church, her black-and-white floral dress swirled in the sea breeze. "*Is* it a date, Deputy Pruitt?" The hem teased at her knees.

"Not if you're going to keep calling me Deputy."

She lifted her chin. "Evy and Charlie, then."

"Charlie and Evy would be more alphabetical." Out of habit, he rested his hands on his hips above where his gun belt usually lay. "Since I know you care so much about that sort of thing."

She bit back a laugh. "There is that."

Tendrils framed her face. The sea wind wasn't much for hairdos.

Resisting the urge to run his fingers through

the silk of her hair, he offered his arm. "Chicken it is."

She slipped her hand through the crook in his elbow. "Who're you calling chicken?"

Later they strolled to the waterfront to gaze over the choppy waves of the harbor to the barrier islands on the horizon. The air held a hint of salt as the wind blew in from the ocean. Late afternoon brought with it a golden hue.

Autumn on the Eastern Shore might become Evy's favorite time of year. And of all the places she'd ever lived, Kiptohanock was her favorite place in the world.

"Favorite movie?" Charlie tapped his finger on his chin. "Let me guess. *Pride and Prejudice.*"

"Which one?"

She laughed when his eyebrows rose.

"There's more than one version?"

"Yes, but—true confession time—" she felt the blush "—I'm a big *Star Trek* fan."

"I like Westerns where the hero triumphs against all odds." He rolled his tongue in his cheek. "As you know from my ringtone, I'm a *Bonanza* kind of guy. *Big Valley* and *Gunsmoke,* too."

"Oh, I loved those as a kid." She rested her

forearms on the top of the seawall overlooking the marina. "I can see that about you."

"And you? Why did you become a librarian?"

Jaunty flags fluttered in the breeze. Boats bobbed in the water. Lazy seagulls cawed above their heads in the blue September sky.

"I like books. I like helping people. Not in a heroic or life-changing way like you. But helping them discover new things about themselves and the world around them. After the torn ligament and surgery, it became obvious I'd never become the prima ballerina I'd wanted to be."

He leaned against the seawall. "A ballerina?"

When he smiled at her like that, it was hard to hold on to her suspicions.

"I didn't know that about you." He propped his elbow on the wall. "I can see it, though. Your hair on top of your head. The tutu. The toe shoes."

"You know about toe shoes?"

"One sister, remember?"

There'd been framed photographs scattered on table surfaces at his house.

"Where is your family? How have I not seen them around town?"

"Dad and Mom bought an RV when he retired. They're at Yellowstone right now. They'll be home for Thanksgiving."

"What about your siblings?"

"Jaxon is career military like my granddad. He doesn't get home much. One brother's a firefighter in Norfolk, and another calls a navy ship home at the moment." Charlie looked at the ground and shuffled his feet. "Anna's husband was also military."

"Was?"

Charlie gave a deep sigh. "Returned from his tour sick. Cancer."

"Is he okay?"

"After a long battle on the home front— waged chiefly by my sweet sister—he died about a year ago." Charlie pushed off from the wall. "Anna became a much-too-young military widow. One of the reasons my dad retired early. So they could be with her in those last days."

"And you hold down the fort till everyone comes home."

"I guess so. Never thought about it that way before."

She wound a strand of hair around her finger. "Such a big family. Sounds wonderful. It was always only my parents and me."

"And your housekeeper."

She exhaled. "My parents meant well. But academia was their life. Grant-funded research. The publish or perish pressure. It was easy for them to get lost in translation, literally."

"For them to get lost or for you?"

She straightened. "They were wonderful in their own way. Wildly eccentric and freethinking, with a circle of eclectic friends. They loved me in the abstract."

Evy touched the frame of her glasses. "They gave me everything money could buy. I think I was a checkmark off a bucket list. They were older than most when they…" She pinched her lips together.

"You don't have to be afraid to tell me anything, Evy. I wouldn't judge you. We each have our own life wounds. The scars we carry."

She edged away from him. "I should go home now."

His face fell. "If I said something—"

"You didn't. I need to do some stuff."

She wasn't sure how the conversation had taken this detour. Her reasons for being in Kiptohanock lay between them like a boulder.

He looked like he didn't believe her. "What about story time tonight? How about I come get you about seven?" Due to the holiday weekend, they had an extra evening with the children, who didn't return to their foster homes until Monday.

"Don't worry about me. I'll drive myself there and see you then."

"You're no trouble. It's on my way." He frowned. "Is something wrong, Evy?"

"Nothing's wrong. See you later."

Confusion flickered across his strong features. "Evy...wait—"

Dodging his hand, with a quick wave she practically ran to where she'd left her car. She spent the rest of the afternoon hunkered in her room at Miss Pauline's, wrestling with the desire to tell Charlie everything.

She liked Charlie. More than a little. And friendships—not to mention relationships—should be based on honesty.

Evy wasn't the sort of person who liked keeping secrets. But other lives and her ability to destroy those lives with one wrong word lay in her hand. It was a responsibility she didn't take lightly. Despite how others might misinterpret her actions, she hadn't come to the Shore to make trouble. Charlie's tangled history with Honey Kole complicated matters and underscored Evy's reservations.

The library board had offered Evy a long-term contract to consider staying permanently as library director. Of all the libraries in which she'd worked, she loved the Kiptohanock library the best. The historic former Victorian home housing the library collection provided plenty of scope for the imagination, as Anne of Green Gables might've said.

She loved the muted, old-fashioned lighting

of the chandeliers. She reveled in the colorful book bindings, side by side like toy soldiers, on the gleaming wooden shelves. She inhaled the waxy aroma of lemon polish. She'd hate leaving this seaside sanctuary.

But more and more, Evy was thinking it wouldn't be such a good idea to stay here. She was in over her head, and she knew it.

As for tonight? She had a story to read. And little girls to cuddle. In what was fast becoming one of her favorite life experiences.

She arrived at the Keller farm alone. Dusk deepened the watery horizon to peach-colored hues laced with lilac and indigo overtones.

Felicia met Evy at her car. "We're going to do a switcheroo tonight."

"A what?"

"I'll help Charlie lead the discussion with the little dudes. And Sawyer is going to share his story with the dudettes after you read the book he picked out." Felicia laughed. "Dudes. Switcheroos. Cowboy life has a way of growing on you."

On the stool between the bunk beds in the girls' cabin, Evy held the book aloft and read aloud from *A Terrible Thing Happened*. With Sawyer there, the girls hadn't changed into their pj's yet. But the girls had belly-flopped onto their bunks as they listened to the story about a boy named Sherman. And what he saw that terrible day.

As she read, something—not exactly a memory—pushed at the edges of Evy's consciousness. She turned the page.

Sherman got nervous. His stomach hurt.

Evy practiced taking a steady breath and turned the page.

Sherman had bad dreams. He was angry and did mean things.

Evy's heart raced.

Then Sherman met Mrs. Maple. He talked about the terrible thing he tried to forget.

Her palms sweated on the book cover. She wiped one hand on the thigh of her jeans. Her hand shook.

Sherman felt much better.

Evy did not. "The End." She closed the book and laid it across her lap.

"When I was a boy, I saw something bad. Something terrible."

Evy's gaze flicked to Sawyer. He sat cross-legged on the rug between the bunk beds. She gripped the book.

She wanted to know. She had waited her entire life to know. But now? Now she was afraid to know the truth.

He laid his palm against the pine board floor. "My mother died on the floor of our kitchen."

Latasha nodded. "Cocaine?"

Rayna, a little girl with a sprinkle of freckles and bright orange hair, jutted her chin. "Meth, maybe."

"Or heroin." That from five-year-old Tonya.

It hurt Evy's heart to realize what unofficial experts these children were. And what hurt even more was the image Sawyer painted with his words.

Sawyer sighed. "My father wasn't a good guy. He yelled a lot. He broke things. I was glad when he went to jail for armed robbery."

Rayna placed her cheek against the blanket.

No child should have to live with those kinds of memories. If Evy hadn't understood she was the fortunate one before, she knew it for a fact now. She got off the stool and moved to sit beside Rayna.

Sawyer took a deep breath. "I never told that story—my story—until I met a real-life good guy. A man by the name of Seth Duer, my future father-in-law. Talking about it made me feel better."

He paused. "Miss Felicia and Miss Shaw are both good listeners. If you ever want to talk to someone."

Tonya's fingers plucked at a loose thread on the hem of her shirt. "My foster mom says there's another father. She says he's good. A father who loves you no matter what."

Sawyer nodded. "I had a lousy father, but Seth helped me find a better one. A father who's always there when I need Him the most. And He gave me a new family. Starting with Seth Duer, then my friend Braeden and finally my precious wife, Honey."

Tonya smiled. "She makes the best pimento cheese sandwiches."

Sawyer laughed. "Yes. She does."

"You're talking about God." Rayna sat up and put her arm around Evy's shoulders. "I've heard of Him. At the church my grandma took me to before she died. Before my sisters and I went to live in different places."

Evy's arm slipped around Rayna's waist. She hugged the little girl close. Latasha plodded across the rug in her stocking feet for a hug of her own.

When Felicia called for lights-out, Evy and Sawyer stepped out onto the cabin stoop.

And something wouldn't allow Evy to walk away to her car. Her time with her brother was destined to be so brief. As had been their childhood together. She might not get another chance to talk one-on-one with him.

"You were scared of your father."

Sawyer's eyes sharpened. "Yes… I was."

She clenched her fists at her sides. "You believed it was your fault."

He didn't blink. "Yes, I did."

"It wasn't." Her heart pounded. "I'm sorry."

His gaze raked over her face, scrutinizing Evy. "Thank you."

A broken image—like shards of glass—flashed across Evy's memory. "He hit you." A statement. Not a question.

Sawyer's eyes bored onto hers. And there, she beheld the truth. "How did you—" He shook his head, as if attempting to dislodge an unsettling idea. "Let me walk you to your car."

Evy stepped off the porch and warred against the temptation to tell Sawyer who she really was. Perhaps he'd be pleased to know her. But what if he'd rather leave his sister and the bad memories in the past? Before she could act on the impulse, Sawyer surprised her.

"How is it that we've known each other such a short time and yet somehow I feel we've known each other far longer?"

Evy's breath quickened. Did he suspect? Had she given herself away? What should she say?

At her silence, he bit his lip. "You've been a great friend to these children. And to me."

Evy swallowed past the emotion clogging her throat. "You've all become a family to me. Like you were talking about earlier with the Duers."

He slowed, matching his longer strides to hers. "All thanks to a good God."

She nodded, not trusting herself to speak.

"Do you believe in God, Miss Shaw?" Sawyer stopped beside her Mini Cooper. "Do you think He's real?"

She looked at Sawyer.

"Yes, I do," she whispered. "And He is very good indeed."

Chapter Seven

The next Thursday afternoon, Charlie ran across Honey coming out of the grocery store. Too late to avoid her, he reached for the bag of groceries in her arms and walked Honey to her car.

"I'm not happy about that Shaw woman spending so much time at the camp on weekends, Charlie."

He set his jaw.

"What were you thinking to bring her out there? And now she's insinuated herself into coming every Saturday."

Honey wasn't being fair.

"Felicia Kerr asked her to take charge of story time." He waited while Honey dug through her purse for her keys. "It was you who pointed out how Evy didn't fit in. Story time is her wheelhouse. She cares about those kids."

Honey clicked her key fob. The car beeped as the door locks clicked upright.

"Evy's not what you're imagining." He balanced the bag on his arm. "There has to be a reasonable explanation. She's a great person."

"Your task, Charlie, was to figure out what her interest is in my family. And to stop her from causing trouble."

Charlie placed the grocery bag inside the trunk. "Evy Shaw has never said or done anything remotely threatening to your family."

Honey slammed the trunk lid shut. She crossed her arms over her expanded belly. "There's something off about her interest in our lives." Her brown eyes filled with tears. "Didn't you see it for yourself on Saturday? Didn't you feel it? Something tying her and Sawyer to each other."

Yes, Charlie had. Only something someone who knew them both would detect. A heightened awareness. A visceral bond.

Honey swiped the moisture from her eyes. "Or do you think I'm just being hormonal?"

Charlie rested his hip against the car. "Have you asked Sawyer about her?"

Honey's mouth quivered. "That was his first time meeting her. But something is going on. I just know it."

Charlie wished the whole subterfuge was

over. He wished he'd never agreed to investigate Evy. He hated lying. Because that's exactly what he was doing by pretending to be her friend so he could unearth Evy's deepest, darkest secrets.

Was he pretending, though? Had it gone far, far beyond that for him? Was he going after the truth for Honey's sake? Or for his own?

He folded his arms across his uniform. "Where was Sawyer stationed before coming to Kiptohanock? And during that three-year period when he—"

"Dumped me." Honey gave him a small smile. "It's okay. You can say it. We were better for being apart for a while so we could be together later. Both of us needed to grow up."

She tapped her finger on her chin, thinking out loud. "Kiptohanock was his first duty station. Then Miami. Followed by San Diego. A joint task force in the Caribbean. Then back to Kiptohanock."

Charlie's gut twisted. Miami. San Diego. In his line of work, he didn't believe in coincidences. "Text me the dates of those assignments."

"Those places mean something to Evy Shaw, don't they? Have you found the connection?"

"Not sure yet. But I think I'm getting close."

Honey touched his arm. "I'm worried about you, too, Charlie. Close is exactly what you seemed to be with that Shaw woman over the weekend. Too close. I don't want to see you get hurt."

Charlie stiffened. "I'm a big boy, Honey. I can take care of myself. No worries."

But that wasn't true. He *was* close. Close to losing his perspective. Beyond losing his objectivity.

Evy Shaw had managed to penetrate his defensive armor. He so wanted to believe in her. But he was afraid of another woman letting him down. Especially Evy.

He planted his hands on his gun belt. "I'll take care of it. I promise, Honey. I won't let you down."

By not trusting Evy, was he letting *her* down? Was he letting himself down? But he reminded himself that he wasn't the only one being secretive.

Honey patted his cheek. "You're one of the good guys, Charlie. I hope you find your happily-ever-after." She grimaced. "Just not with the likes of the secretive librarian."

Evy couldn't believe her eyes. *Her* Charlie and Honey Kole in the Four Corners Shopping Center parking lot. She made a face. He wasn't *her* Charlie.

"Coupons?"

Evy refocused on the cashier. "Uh, no." Her eyes cut to the plate-glass windows.

"That'll be ten dollars and seventy-six cents."

Evy watched as Charlie placed Honey's groceries in her trunk. A seed of suspicion grew in Evy's mind. Why were they together in the parking lot? What was going on? Had she been wrong to trust Charlie, to reveal as much of herself as she had?

"Ma'am? If you'd just swipe your card and punch Yes into the keypad?"

"What?" Evy dragged her attention to the cashier. "Oh."

She fumbled inside her purse for her wallet. There were exclamations of annoyance from the customers behind her in line. Flustered, she dropped her credit card onto the floor.

Crouching, she stole another look at the parking lot. Honey and Charlie were talking beside Honey's car. Really close. In that way people have when what they're saying is private and they don't want to be overheard.

"Any day, lady…" Judging from his accent, a 'come here. Like herself.

She scrounged for the credit card. Where—?

"Let me help, Evy."

A pair of hot-pink sneakers moved into her line of vision. And Dixie dropped to her knees.

She nudged Evy's foot. "Under there, sugar. You're stepping on it."

"Oh." Evy crab-walked a step and picked the card off the linoleum. Cheeks flushed, she got to her feet.

The cashier reached over the checkout counter and ran the card through the machine herself.

"Sorry," Evy murmured to the line of customers.

"It's about time."

"Some of us got stuff to do, lady."

Dixie rose with an ease that belied her forty-plus years and glared at the customers in line. "Some of us need to take a chill pill and get a life."

Evy bit her lip and keyed the green button as instructed. Her gaze strayed to the window. Charlie was looming over Honey.

"Your receipt...ma'am?"

Evy took the slip of paper from the cashier. The woman thrust a plastic bag in her direction. But Evy's gaze flew to the window again.

The man behind her, in Bermuda shorts and knee-high socks, groaned. "Do you mind, lady?"

Dixie steered Evy toward the exit. "Come on, sugar."

But when Honey touched Charlie's face, Evy put on the brakes. She couldn't go out there.

Not while they were…while he… Evy's heart pounded.

Though Honey had moved on with her life, had Charlie? Was he still nursing his broken heart? Would he ever be able to move on? Especially with someone like Evy, Honey Kole's polar opposite?

"When she first met Sawyer Kole, Honey worked at the Sandpiper. Did you know that?"

Dixie stared out the window, having followed the direction of Evy's gaze.

Evy lifted her chin. "You two must've been friends."

Dixie laughed. "You make it sound so improbable anyone would ever want to be friends with Honey."

Evy remained silent.

"Honey's a nice person. As are you." Dixie wrapped her arm around Evy's tense shoulders. "When the two of you aren't working at cross-purposes. But I understand. I remember what it's like to fall in love. The terror. The—"

"I'm not falling in love."

Customers veered around them. The electric doors whooshed open and shut. Evy's hand knotted around the grocery bag.

Dixie sniffed. "I never believed those two belonged together. And I was right. Only thing they had in common was a desire to remain on the Shore." She cocked her head. "Charlie's one of the good guys. Just like Sawyer."

Evy fidgeted.

"Charlie got his pride hurt with Honey, not his heart." Dixie wagged her finger. "But I'm thinking since he met a certain librarian, he's moved on in more ways than one."

Evy studied her shoes. "Doesn't seem that way to me."

Dixie squared her shoulders. "Appearances don't always tell the whole truth, sugar."

Charlie left Honey and strolled toward his patrol vehicle. Honey pulled out onto the highway, headed south toward Kiptohanock.

Dixie readjusted the strap of her purse over her shoulder. "Ready for book club tonight?"

Evy let out the breath she hadn't realized she'd been holding. "I've kept you from making your own purchases."

"I'll head down the aisle in a minute. But when I spotted you in line, you appeared to need help."

"Thanks for being my friend." She watched Charlie's cruiser head north. "Sometimes, though, appearances are exactly what you believe." She sighed.

Dixie shook her head. "Don't give up on our handsome deputy yet."

Later at the library, Evy toted the metal can

to the front door to water the red geraniums on the porch. Careful not to spill anything on the hardwood floors inside, she stepped over the threshold. But the spout wobbled.

Droplets spattered the wide-planked porch. She'd filled the watering can too full. She tottered over to the first step and bent over the urn. She needed both hands to hold the watering can steady. Footsteps thudded on the sidewalk.

"We're closed," she called out. "We open tomorrow morning at ten."

"Good to know, but that's not why I'm here."

She raised her gaze. Slowly. Onto a pair of scuffed, well-worn boots. Cowboy boots.

"Miss Shaw."

In a flannel shirt and jeans covered in what appeared to be wood shavings, Sawyer Kole stood on the sidewalk. Her sidewalk. The library sidewalk.

Her mouth went dry. "M-Mr. Kole."

She remembered then that he worked weekdays at the construction site of the new aquatic center on the outskirts of Kiptohanock.

His eyes twinkled. "Maybe you could call me Sawyer?"

She nodded. Her head bobbed like a marionette on a string. And he, the puppet master.

"Evy," she whispered.

His eyes were the same light blue she remembered. She'd been afraid he'd remember her. But he didn't. She told herself it was okay. Better for him not to remember.

"Evy it is."

She swallowed. Tried not to stare, but she couldn't seem to look away. She wanted to memorize his features. Commit them to memory. Because all too soon, she'd never see him again.

Which was the way it should be. Tears burned at the backs of her eyelids. She'd need to live off these moments with him for the rest of her life.

He tilted his head. "You seem to have a heart for what we're trying to accomplish with the foster kids."

Evy couldn't let this chance go by without conveying a small sense of what she thought of Sawyer Kole's character. "But it takes a special person—like you—to have created a place for them to reconnect with their families."

The late-afternoon sun glinted off his blond hair. "I did what I had to do. What I felt was right. After everything God has done for me. Kiptohanock. Honey. Now the baby…"

His eyes bored into Evy's. "To help someone else the way I wish my sister and I had been…" A vein pulsed in his clenched jaw.

Though he didn't recognize her, Sawyer hadn't forgotten his sister. Evy imagined her heart might burst. Out of the pain of the past, something good like this foster kids' camp had come.

And Evy reckoned if she died right now, she'd die happy. 'Cause she knew at long last Sawyer was okay. More than okay.

He'd found a real home here. Everything she ever wanted for him. She clutched the watering can.

It was time. Time to go. But because of Charlie, it was going to be harder than she'd bargained for. But still the right thing for her to do. The only thing for her to do.

Sawyer stuck his hands in his jeans pockets. "Guess Honey's not the only one with prenatal hormones." He blew out a breath, as uncomfortable with emotion as a certain Accomack County deputy sheriff she knew. "Anyway…"

Those two had far more in common than they supposed. Both were good men. Honorable. Admirable in their vocations and callings. And she loved them both.

She sucked in a breath. That couldn't be true. Could it?

"I didn't like seeing you so afraid of horses, Evy. Did something happen when you were younger to make you scared of them?"

She set the watering can onto the top step. For once, almost eye level with Sawyer. "No. Just haven't been around them much."

"Horses were my best friends for years." He grinned. "Until I met a honey-blonde innkeeper."

This was surreal. For so long, she'd imagined herself and Sawyer talking. As if nothing had ever come between them.

"Could you come out early on Saturday, Evy? I could give you and the other kids who are afraid a private lesson."

This was not a good idea. She gulped. For more than one reason.

"Me? Why?"

He blinked. Her question had thrown him. Confusion flickered in his eyes. "Maybe because I hate to admit defeat. And I hate for you not to know the pleasure horses bring to life."

"Why does it matter? About me?"

He kicked a pebble with the toe of his boot. "I'm thinking if we did a smaller group, by the final camp weekend, it'd make a difference for us."

Us…and he hadn't answered her question.

"You don't need me to accomplish that with the children."

He stood there a moment, framing a reply. "Latasha and the others really bonded with you. If they saw you overcoming your fears, it'd be an example for them to move past their own fears. And move past more than their fear of riding."

Accepting his offer could prove to be a huge mistake. Who was she kidding? *Would* prove to be a huge mistake. But he'd chosen to ignore her attempt to offer him an out. Which told her a lot.

While he might not remember her, he felt the connection, too. Didn't understand it. But felt it nonetheless.

She had committed to spearheading story time for the duration of the pilot program. And she'd never been the kind of person to renege on her word. Especially concerning something she believed in with all her heart.

An excuse? Sure. But she'd seize any reason to justify delaying her departure by a few more weeks.

She took a breath. "I can be there before the library opens for the day. Seven-thirty."

"Really?" As if he hadn't believed she'd do it. But as if he hoped… He leaned against the pillar. "Thanks, Evy. It'll be fun. I promise."

What it was, was incredibly foolish. And self-ish on her part. Increasing exponentially the chance of exposure. But despite what her good sense shouted, she wasn't ready to say goodbye.

Not to Kiptohanock. Not to Sawyer. Not to Charlie.

Which made Evy Shaw perhaps the biggest idiot of all.

Chapter Eight

Thursday afternoon, outside the Sandpiper Café, in what had become a habit of late, Charlie peered across the square toward the library. At Sawyer Kole and Evy on the library steps.

All the breath went out of Charlie. Something familiar about the pair of them niggled at the back of his mind. Some similarity between them. The hair? The eyes? Were they—?

No, he was being fanciful. And deputy sheriffs didn't live long on the job by being fanciful. Still, the notion shook him.

He was the one losing it. Unable to trust his legs, Charlie leaned against his truck. Couldn't be. But what was up with Evy's fascination with Sawyer Kole? Was Charlie being used to further some secret agenda?

Charlie flung the white bakery box through the open window of the truck. He scrubbed his hand over his beard shadow. What was wrong with *him* that he always wanted what he couldn't have?

Detoured from his mission by Honey at the grocery store parking lot, as a last resort he'd placed a call to Dixie. Who met him at the closed diner, which only served breakfast and lunch. Where he purchased a homemade coconut cake. His contribution to book club tonight.

Evy Shaw was going to make him crazy. He hated secrets. After their Sunday afternoon together, he'd started to believe this relationship would be different. That *she* would be different.

Which only proved he was a bigger idiot than he'd believed possible. Therefore, he wasn't in the best of moods. After an hour of pacing inside his house, he changed into comfortable jeans and his Virginia Tech sweatshirt.

Cake box in hand, he stalked around the square toward the library. Trying to work off misplaced energy. To no avail.

In truth—something Evy Shaw apparently knew nothing about—he was spoiling for a fight. He clomped up the steps.

He was reaching for the door handle when, midmotion, Evy threw open the door. Her cheeks lifted. Her eyes brightened.

Charlie scowled. To look at her, you'd have thought she was tickled to see him. Which proved just how wrong appearances could be. How wrong a guy like him could be.

"Hey, Charlie."

She almost made him believe she'd been watching for him. But he was on to her. What kind of a chump did she think he was? He clutched the box to his chest.

"You brought dessert. Aren't you going to say hello?"

She twirled a strand of blond hair around her finger. The picture of wistful insecurity. Unsure of herself.

But she knew exactly what she was doing. It was a game he was tired of playing.

Charlie thrust the box at her. She staggered a step back in those heels of hers. She had such pretty ankles, he thought, not for the first time.

He glared. She'd probably worn the fluttery pink blouse on purpose. Calculated its effect on him.

She gave him a nervous smile. "Are you okay, Charlie? You seem, uh…"

"Wound a little tight?" he growled. "Wonder why."

She stepped aside to let him pass. Holding the box in the crook of her arm, she closed the heavy oak door behind him. He marched past the reception desk, beyond the staircase to the meeting room.

"You're the first to arrive." She staccato-stepped to keep pace with his long strides. "I'm glad."

"Why?"

Evy inhaled as she placed the box on the burgundy tablecloth. "Is that coconut?"

She lifted the lid and frowned. "Did you have an accident with the cake, Charlie?"

His gaze moved from her face to the cake. One lop-sided layer had slid halfway off the bottom layer. A victim of an up-close-and-personal encounter with the floorboard of his truck.

"Maybe we'll leave the cake as-is in the box. People can serve themselves. I'll get the plates."

"Why are you glad to see me?"

Evy headed to the small kitchen. "I hoped it would give us a chance to talk. I haven't seen…" The timbre of her voice changed. "I mean, we haven't talked since Sunday." She blushed. "I had a wonderful time. A great afternoon."

It had been a wonderful day. The best. Or so he'd believed until about five o'clock this afternoon.

He'd spent far too many sleepless nights this week thinking about seeing her again. But conflicted by the secrets he sensed she kept.

Not sure if he should trust her. Not sure if he should trust any woman again. Not sure if he wanted to open himself to further hurt.

Because in the short but intense time he'd known Evy Shaw—whoever she was, whatever she was after—he'd come to realize she possessed the power to truly hurt him. In a way Honey had never been able. Like getting shot while not wearing any Kevlar. A deathblow from Evy from which his heart might never recover.

Charlie bristled. "You want to talk? Then talk."

Her smile flickered. "I—I missed you." A little-girl pang in her voice.

Charlie looked into her eyes then. That was a mistake. He started to go under. Drowning in her gaze. A willing victim.

She wore her heart in her eyes. Somebody ought to tell her that. Before…before she blew her own con.

He hardened his heart. "Did you? Miss me?"

The light in her eyes dimmed. He felt like a first-class heel. She placed the plates beside the cake box.

She bit her lip. "I forgot the napkins."

And as she moved once again toward the kitchen, he felt rather than saw her do that thing. The shrinking, the pulling back, the withdrawing. Raising the drawbridge. Because of him.

He almost reached out to her. Almost. But

then Mrs. Davenport and the other ladies arrived. And the moment was lost.

Charlie was afraid suddenly that something much more precious had been lost, as well. He hated the suspicion consuming him.

Her gaze darting from him to Evy, Dixie filled the awkward, tense moment with inane chatter. The way only Dixie could. But she was deeper than most people realized.

There was a lot more beneath the peroxide-blond perm and shoot-from-the-hip, gum-chewing stereotype that Dixie cultivated. She and Bernie had found each other later in life. Past the childbearing years.

The endless crocheted baby blankets she made in her off hours for the neonatal unit at the hospital were a quiet testament to how empty her arms felt. So she adopted strays. Offered Charlie bottomless cups of coffee at the diner since the Honey fiasco and his parents hit the road, too often out of reach.

Had she decided to adopt Evy, too? Who, perhaps, needed a mother like Dixie most of all.

Evy fought back tears as she called the book club to order. Something was terribly wrong with Charlie. Something terribly wrong between them.

If only she knew what she'd done. If only she

knew how to fix it. To return to the easygoing camaraderie they'd shared last weekend.

She'd been disappointed when he didn't call this week. Leaving her open to raking doubts, striking at the most inopportune moments.

Like anytime she drew a breath. But there'd been a string of burglaries in the usually tranquil county. She figured he'd been busy at work. Mrs. Davenport—who had her finger on the pulse of Kiptohanock via a police scanner— kept her informed.

Evy cleared her throat. "Anyone want to kick off the discussion tonight? What were your thoughts on our reading selection this week?"

Avoiding eye contact with Charlie, she glanced around the semicircle of women. Were any of them what they seemed? More than the image they projected to the outside world?

The young Coastie wife, Kelly, separated from her family by military life, was lonely. Frail Mrs. Evans, whose children and grandchildren lived off-Shore. Ashley, setting aside a flourishing career to fulfill her most important assignment thus far—being a mother. But who still craved more intellectual stimulation than wiping noses and changing diapers every day.

And how many took the time to look beyond Mrs. Davenport's starched exterior to understand how desperately empty was the life she lived in the brick mansion on Seaside Road? Did anyone bother to look beyond her arm's-length snobbery to the lonely hours she filled with books and meddling in other people's business? While her husband did whatever it was he did so successfully somewhere else?

But Evy knew. Because more often than not, she learned more than just people's favorite authors when they wandered the stacks at the library. People came searching for more than a good book. Old Mrs. Beal, the previous librarian, told her it would be so. And it was.

So like Mrs. Beal before her, she'd given the only thing she had to offer. A listening ear. Her time. And words of kindness.

Evy had created a small community within the library walls of Kiptohanock. Not only for herself but also for others. A safe haven among her beloved books.

Was it enough? She risked a glance at Charlie's shuttered countenance. It used to be enough.

Mrs. Davenport, ramrod straight in the high-backed chair, balanced a plate on her immaculately tailored slacks. "I think at the heart of this novel lies tension. A tension between what is concealed and what is revealed."

Charlie's mouth flattened. "You mean secrets."

Evy's gaze flitted to Charlie. "Aren't people

allowed to have private places within themselves that they share with no one else?"

"I think secrets destroy people." Resting on his thigh, his hand flexed. "And relationships."

Jolene raised the coffeepot. "Anybody want decaf?"

"Thanks, but I'm fine." Charlie glared at Evy. "Truly."

Dixie cut her eyes at Charlie and then at Evy. "In the novel, Elinor goes to great lengths to keep her feelings for Edward concealed beneath a cool exterior to protect their relationship from outside damage."

Charlie cocked his head. "In refusing to tell the truth, Elinor did that anyway."

Evy's stomach turned over. "Did something bad happen at work today, Charlie?" she blurted out.

Their gazes locked. No one said anything.

Mrs. Davenport wiped the edge of her mouth with a napkin. "The secrets were eventually revealed."

Charlie's nostrils flared. "They always are."

"Intentionally or not." Kelly took a bite of cake. "This is good. Who brought the cake?"

His mouth thinned. "Unintentional revelations often prove the most damaging. And painful."

Evy's chest rose and fell. "Everything's about proof with you, isn't it, Charlie?"

His eyes narrowed. "Since that's what I do, Evy."

Ashley exchanged a worried glance with Mrs. Evans. "In the beginning of the novel, Marianne believed only in love at first sight. That second attachments weren't possible."

Dixie chewed her lip. "I think Austen shows through Marianne's subsequent marriage to Colonel Brandon that people can indeed start over." She fingered the plastic bangles on her wrist. "Bernie and I are proof of that."

Proof? Evy withheld a sigh. *Et tu, Dixie?*

Evy lifted her chin. "So real, lasting love means loving only one person, Charlie?"

He broadened his shoulders. "Do you live your life with more sense or more sensibility, Evy?"

She planted her feet on the floor. "Do you ever wish you could live your life differently, Deputy Pruitt?"

A muscle thrummed in his cheek. "Do you, Miss Shaw?"

She stared into his eyes. "Is something wrong? Is there something you need to say?"

"Nothing's wrong." He smirked. "Is there something you'd like to say?"

Evy steeled herself. "Do you believe, if given

the opportunity, that Marianne would've re-united with Willoughby, her first love? Would you, Charlie?"

"A do-over?" He hunched forward. "I think life rarely gives second chances, Evy."

His hazel eyes had gone hard. What had she done? Why was he so upset with her?

The wall clock ticked. The refrigerator hummed. Jolene opened her mouth, maybe thought better of it and closed her mouth again.

"I think…" Dixie waited until she had everyone's attention "…that passion for life—or sensibility, as Austen coins it—does not have to equal one love over the other."

Peggy, a retired math teacher, nodded. "In my experience, the most remarkable loves are characterized by selfless choices that point others to the greatest love of all."

Old Mrs. Evans smiled. "Loving others more than you love yourself."

With effort, Evy broke the laser-like intensity of Charlie's gaze. He folded his arms across his chest. She knotted her fingers in her lap. For the life of her, she didn't know what to say. Couldn't speak past the tears clogging her throat.

Mrs. Davenport rose. "Excellent discussion." She briefly touched Evy's shoulder, interrupting her miserable contemplation of Charlie across the circle. "I think we've explored this topic as far as we can take it. At least for tonight."

The grande dame pursed her lips. "Cake, anyone?"

Chapter Nine

Book club had gotten entirely out of hand.

That night, Charlie lay awake, tormented. He couldn't go on this way. Feeling as he did for Evy. Doubting himself and his instincts. Doubting her.

When further sleep eluded him, he gave in to the inevitable and padded downstairs to reheat a cup of day-old coffee. He grimaced at the bitter taste. Cream and sugar didn't help. He set it aside.

At loose ends, he hunched over the kitchen island and riffled through the folder he'd started on Evy. A folder on someone who was supposed to be his friend. Suddenly Charlie was sick of his own secrecy. Sick of himself.

What right did he have to question Evy when his own conduct wasn't exactly above reproach? Yet his training forced him to check the dates of Sawyer's duty stations against the papers his detective friend had emailed regarding Evy's employment history. Same towns, but different dates.

No overlap. Not a match. His spirits lifted.

Until he noticed that in each city, Evy arrived six to eight months after Sawyer departed. And his instincts, which made Charlie a good cop, vibrated.

If it had happened once, he might have believed it was a coincidence. Three times, no way. It appeared as if she'd been tracking Sawyer Kole. Charlie bit the inside of his cheek so hard he tasted blood.

The dates revealed a pattern of behavior. As if she'd been searching for Sawyer Kole. Only to be two steps behind. Stalking the ex-Coastie. Arriving at each city a little too late each and every time.

Fatigue overwhelmed Charlie. He rested his arms on top of the paperwork and laid down his head. Trust came so hard for him. He wanted to believe in her. Despite the evidence, he wanted so much to believe Evy Shaw was who and what she claimed to be.

Why had he agreed to start this underhanded business with Honey? Why had he continued it, long after his heart told him to trust Evy? Especially when the only one who'd abused his trust hadn't been Evy Shaw but Honey.

Didn't loyalty to Evy outweigh any other factor? Hadn't she earned the right to be trusted? Was his trust in Honey misguided and misplaced?

He squeezed his eyes shut. He hated this. He despised himself. For the first time, he regretted the profession he'd chosen, the oath he'd taken to serve and protect. He hated what the job— and pride—had done to him in terms of cynical disbelief. What it had cost his faith.

But if not for his investigation, would he have ever walked into the Kiptohanock library and met Evy? Despite everything, his life was far richer from knowing her. He'd started to believe again. Truly believe in a lot of things, not merely giving lip service to faith on Sunday morning.

Was this part of some plan I don't understand, God? Have I ruined everything with Evy? What should I do? I'm so sorry for not seeking Your wisdom first. Please help me make this right.

He must have drifted off to sleep. Because the next thing he knew, ice fell with a clatter from the ice maker inside the refrigerator. He jerked upright on the stool.

And awoke knowing what he had to do. He'd behaved like an idiot. No excuses. He had to act like the friend he was supposed to be. A friend to Evy. No matter whether or not God intended anything else ever to develop between him and the most enchanting librarian he'd ever known.

Charlie's mouth curved. He could hear Evy's amusement in his head. Evy was the *only* librarian he'd ever known.

There was probably a reasonable explanation as to why Evy Shaw always found a job in a city Sawyer just happened to live in first.

Charlie stared at next week's book club selection where he'd tossed it on the counter after tonight's meeting. *Northanger Abbey*. Marvelous. He made a face.

He couldn't wait to crack the spine. Right... Still, he'd enjoyed the whole Austen club more than he'd have ever believed.

With dawn streaking the sky, he might as well dive in. Further sleep wasn't an option. He'd be dead on his feet during his shift tomorrow—he took another glance out the window—today, that is. He'd apologize to Evy first chance he got on his morning break. He flipped open the book.

Catherine Morland's over-the-top imagination made him laugh. Seeing a mystery where there was none. He frowned. Had he done the same with Evy?

And he wasn't sure he cared for the hero of the story, Henry. Or his sometimes patronizing attitude toward the younger heroine. Had Charlie misjudged Evy and her motivations?

He'd gotten well into volume two of the book when his cell phone buzzed. It skipped and skidded across the granite countertop. Glancing at the text, he put the book down. A situation had arisen. He'd been called in to work early.

Further reading—and an overdue apology— would have to wait. He pushed back the stool. It scudded over the hardwood floor. This was shaping up to be a potentially exhausting day.

He put everything else—including Evy—into the box in his mind labeled Not Work. Same as every cop he knew. Like his dad had taught him.

To do anything else dulled his senses and put his life in jeopardy.

Evy was mad.

She was so mad, she wished libraries still used those rubber stamps for due dates.

Stamping something, anything, would have been so satisfying right now. Mainly though, she would have liked a chance to thump Charlie Pruitt upside his hard, stubborn head.

Instead she ripped the slip of paper from the printer. She thrust the printout of due dates at Agnes Parks, the preacher's wife.

Agnes gave Evy an uncertain smile. "Is everything okay, Evy?"

"Everything is great," she huffed. "Jim-dandy. Outstanding. Magnifi—"

"Good." Agnes backed away, her eyes never leaving Evy's face. "Good to hear." She groped for the door. "Bye now."

Evy sagged onto the checkout desk. One more person to apologize to. After she found out what was eating Charlie and apologized for whatever it was she'd done to tick him off so royally.

Mrs. Davenport's bulk filled the vestibule. "Evy." She quivered in her stylish designer flats. "I was listening to the police scanner. There's been an incident."

A sinking feeling in the pit of Evy's stomach threatened to swallow her whole. She was thankful she and Mrs. Davenport had the library to themselves.

"What's happened? Is Charlie involved?"

"A Shore Stop convenience store robbery over the state line in Maryland. The police chase spilled over into our county. And yes, Charlie is involved."

Evy's knees went weak. Of course Deputy Charlie Pruitt was involved. It's who he was. What he did. Protecting and serving the citizens of Accomack County.

Mrs. Davenport drew herself up, arms crossed over her ponderous chest. "Which is why I came straight here. I knew you'd want to know." Her blue-green eyes glinted. "You do want to know, don't you?"

Evy nodded. Thinking of Sunday afternoon along the waterfront, she swallowed. A perfect day. A glorious day.

When the world appeared bright with possibilities. With hope and a future she hadn't dared allow herself to believe might exist for someone like her. The girl who hid behind books and library walls.

"Just wanted to clarify." Mrs. Davenport pursed her lips. "After the ridiculous way the two of you behaved last night."

Why hadn't she understood the real life-and-death stress Charlie's job entailed? Why had she never stopped to consider the danger he endured on a daily basis? And the toll it had to take on him—physically, emotionally, relationally.

Evy sank onto the stool behind the desk. "What's happened to Charlie?"

"The Accomack sheriff and deputies were in pursuit of two suspects in a blue Taurus. State troopers established a roadblock close to the Northampton County line."

Evy's gaze cut behind Mrs. Davenport to the framed map of the Eastern Shore on the wall. The highway split the two-county Virginia portion of the Eastern Shore in half.

A dividing line, parting bayside from seaside. The highway connected the small hamlets like a concrete ribbon. From the border of Maryland to the end of the highway at the Chesapeake Bay-Bridge Tunnel.

Keep him safe, Lord. Please don't let anything happen to Charlie. Please, God...

Mrs. Davenport came around behind the desk. She put her arm around Evy's shoulders.

Evy blinked at Mrs. Davenport. "But he's okay, right? He has to be okay."

Fear coiled in her belly. She couldn't seem to catch her breath. She was afraid to move. To breathe. To think.

"Shots were fired. There was an accident involving Charlie's cruiser." Mrs. Davenport's chin trembled. "An ambulance was quickly on the scene."

"No..." Evy sagged against her. *Please, God, no.* She squeezed her eyes shut.

Mrs. Davenport captured Evy's face between her hands. "Look at me."

Evy opened her eyes.

"Don't assume the worst. They're transporting him to the hospital. That's all the information I have."

"But suppose..." Tears fell unheeded on Evy's cheeks. "Suppose he's already...?"

She couldn't—wouldn't—say those words.

Could she have come this close to happiness only to see it snatched away?

Mrs. Davenport hugged Evy close. "He's strong. And you must be strong for him. You need to go to Riverside Hospital. Be there for him. He'll need you, Evy."

She withdrew from Mrs. Davenport's embrace and started for the door only to stop short. "But the library... I can't—"

"Yes, you can." Mrs. Davenport fingered the pearls at her throat. "As the chairwoman of the Kiptohanock Library Committee, I'm sure I can check out a few books and keep the lights burning for our patrons as long as I'm needed."

"Are you sure?"

Mrs. Davenport fluttered her hands toward the door. "Go. Just go."

Evy grabbed her purse. Prayers, a litany of petitions for Charlie's well-being, flooded her mind.

"Keep your cell phone on." Mrs. Davenport took Evy's customary spot behind the checkout desk. "I'm putting in a call to Jolene. She'll have answers neither you or I will have access to. I'll have her meet you in ER and take care of you from that end."

Evy stumbled toward the door. Her hand on the knob, she paused. "Thank you, Mrs. Davenport." She fought to keep from losing it again. "For everything." She pushed her glasses higher onto the bridge of her nose as she ran out of the library.

Chapter Ten

Throwing herself into her car, Evy hastened out of Kiptohanock. Down Seaside Road, she clattered over the tiny bridge at Quinby. Pulling onto Highway 13, she broke without compunction every speed limit on the way to the hospital.

She figured every law enforcement officer was probably further south, mopping up the situation. But she couldn't have been more mistaken.

Evy barreled into the emergency room. A sea of Accomack County Sheriff's Department uniforms filled the waiting area. She halted her headlong flight and chewed her lip.

The smell of antiseptic flooded her senses. Her gaze swept the waiting room. Before her, a gauntlet of khaki brown. State trooper gray, too. Where was Jolene?

One of the officers—a state trooper—broke away from the pack and came toward Evy.

Tensing, she widened her stance even with her hips. This was America. A free country. And nobody was throwing her out of here. Not until she'd made sure Charlie was okay.

The trooper—in his late twenties like Charlie—smiled. "Are you Evy Shaw?"

"Yes…"

Her eyes darted to the others, their faces impassive. Except for a mutual leashed anger. And concern. Adrenaline vibrated between the men and women.

"How do you—"

"I'm Thad Walters. Charlie and I partner sometimes on interagency situations. He told me about you."

She blinked against the harsh glare of fluorescent lights. Her heart hammered. Charlie talked about her to his friends? And she was ridiculously pleased.

"How did you know it was me?"

Another smile. "He described you to a T. The heels. The skirt. The glasses. The ponytail." Officer Walters steered her toward the others. "How pretty you are. And smart."

The circle opened. Admitting her as a member. And closed again.

"Is Charlie…? Can you tell me…?" Tears

pricked the edges of her lashes. "He's not dead. Don't tell me he's dead."

"No, ma'am. We're waiting for the nurse to come out of the examining room. But he was conscious when the EMTs arrived."

She put a shaky hand to her throat.

"You need to sit down. Before you fall down." Walters eased Evy into a chair and then leaned against the nearby wall. The at-ease posture so reminiscent of Charlie that her breath caught. Perhaps no one in law enforcement did stand up straight.

"We established a roadblock at the bridge." A Northampton deputy rested his hands on his gun belt. "No way we were letting them off the peninsula. Not on our watch."

Thad Walters nodded. "Charlie's car took the lead. And the morons—"

"I believe you mean the alleged morons, Officer Walters." An older man's lips quirked.

Judging from the pins on his shirt, someone higher in the law enforcement food chain. And then Evy recognized him from his picture in newspaper articles. The Accomack County sheriff.

Walters rolled his tongue in his cheek. "My bad. The *alleged* morons fired. Took out one of Charlie's tires. At the high rate of speed, the vehicle flipped—"

Evy closed her eyes at the image of a car hurtling out of control. Of Charlie wrestling with the steering wheel. The vehicle, with him inside, rolling over and over.

There would've been sounds of grinding metal. The crashing thud of impact as the patrol car settled upside down on the asphalt. An air bag deploying.

Despite his toughness, he must have been so scared. She was so scared for him. For the first time in her life, Evy wished she didn't have such a vivid imagination. That she hadn't gone through a phase of reading police thrillers five years ago.

"You guys should work on your bedside manner."

At Jolene's voice, the men and women—including Evy—rose from the chairs.

Evy elbowed the taller men out of her way. "Jolene?"

In her green hospital scrubs, Jolene exuded her own authority. They were in her jurisdiction now. "He's going to be okay."

Evy clutched the strap of her shoulder bag. *Thank you. Oh, thank You, God.*

The officers exhaled. Several lifted their faces to the ceiling. Their lips worked silently.

Jolene gave her a hug. "He's blessed. No spinal trauma. Some bruised ribs, which will make him wonder if he's going to die after all. Possibly a slight concussion. After examining the results of the MRI and X-rays, the doctor is writing a prescription for pain medication."

"You're sure he's okay?"

Dixie and the love of her life, Bernie, charged full tilt into the waiting room. The Sandpiper waitress shouldered through the band of brothers. Apologizing on her behalf, Bernie, a middle-aged engineer from Wallops Island, followed in her wake, gripping a cell phone.

"One morning off," Dixie huffed. "And chaos erupts in my absence. Bernie and I were out on the boat and didn't hear the news till I returned my books to the library. Mrs. Davenport said to tell you she's fine. And I promised to give her the details. Which would be what, Jolene?"

"A possible concussion. He'll need monitoring for twenty-four hours." Jolene shrugged. "But otherwise nothing to keep him from returning to the chip-on-his-handsome-shoulder Charles Pruitt we've come to know and love."

Evy sank into the chair.

Walters turned his hat around in his hands. "Is he okay for company?"

"Only a few while we're putting together his discharge papers."

Walters, the sheriff and the Northampton deputy moved toward the curtained examination rooms at the end of the hall. The others disbanded. The exit doors opened and shut.

The brisk seaside air of September flicked across Evy's skin. She shivered. "You're letting him go home, Jolene?" she whispered. "Is that wise?"

"Like mere mortals could keep SuperDeputy here?" Jolene rocked in her rubber-soled mules. "What do we know? We're just medical professionals." She rolled her eyes. "He wants to go back to work."

At Evy's motion of protest, Jolene squeezed her arm.

"Don't worry. Not happening. Doctor's orders. But he can go home as long as someone volunteers to watch him for complications. And makes sure he doesn't overdo it."

The sheriff and Charlie's friend, Walters, returned to the waiting area.

"Anybody ready for the challenge?" Jolene did a slow pivot of the remaining members of law enforcement. "Any of you brave boys and girls in blue? Anybody? But Evy's got first dibs. How about it, darlin'?"

Evy set her jaw. "He'll behave on my watch. I'll see to it."

Jolene gave Evy a small two-fingered salute. "Thank you for your service."

Dixie smoothed Evy's hair. "You get him settled at home. Bernie and I will cover the night watch."

Bernie's bald head glistened in the fluorescent lighting. "Wouldn't be proper for a single gal like you to be at his house alone with him at night." He glanced at the screen on his cell phone.

Evy raised her eyebrows. "In his condition, I hardly think he's likely to besmirch my honor."

Dixie patted Evy's purse. "Who says we were talking about him, sugar?"

Evy laughed. As Dixie had meant for her to.

"Did I ever tell you, Dixie, how much it means to me that you've been my friend? In spite of your longstanding relationship with certain others."

"Honey has her sisters. You've had nobody but me for a long time." Dixie sniffed. "Too long a time, I expect."

Bernie's gaze dropped to his phone. "Dixie called Charlie's mother. Expect a phone call tonight. His brother is driving over from Norfolk after his shift at the firehouse to ride herd on Charlie for the weekend. He'll be here at first light."

Dixie checked her lipstick in her compact mirror. "Expect a phone call from all of 'em. Only one I didn't get, of course, was the Pruitt

currently floating somewhere in the Mediterranean."

She cocked her head at Bernie. "Speaking
of the Mediterranean, our sixth anniversary is
coming up, Bernard."

Bernie raised his eyebrows. "You bring the
sunscreen, and I'll bring the snorkel gear?"

"Sounds like a plan."

Bernie and Dixie smiled at each other. True
love. The kind that lasted.

An improbable match—the serious, analyti-
cal, never-married engineer and the seemingly
ditzy, never-met-a-stranger waitress. But theirs
was the real deal. Evy should be so lucky—no,
make that blessed.

Bernie and Dixie went in to see Charlie next
after Evy begged off. "I'll wait. You go ahead."

After what happened last night, would Charlie be pleased to see her? Did he even want to
see her?

She freed her hair from the confines of the ponytail. Agitated, she raked her fingers through
her hair. But oh, how she longed to see him. If
nothing else, to reassure herself Charlie was really okay.

When Bernie and Dixie emerged from the
curtained-off cubicle, Evy pushed to her feet.
And took a deep breath.

* * *

Where were his pants?

Charlie tried sitting up in the hospital bed. At the throbbing stab of pain, he gasped and fell onto the pillow. The room swam.

He waited for the wooziness to subside. He appreciated the well wishes of his colleagues and friends. In the small Eastern Shore community, everyone knew everybody. Or knew somebody who knew everybody else.

Word of his accident had spread fast. Orderlies he'd known since his football days at Nandua High popped their heads around the curtain to check his status. Therapists who knew his mother stopped to say hello. It appeared that everybody was worried about his well-being.

Except for the one person he wanted to see the most. As the minutes slid by, she was apparently the only one who didn't care if he was dead or alive. The curtain twitched.

A mirage? He blinked to make sure.

Her hands on her hips, Evy Shaw was a sight for sore eyes in her black pencil skirt and starched sea-blue blouse. Her hair, interestingly enough, had come loose from her usual ponytail. It billowed around her shoulders. Framing her face.

He'd never seen Evy with her hair down. He

would've never suspected how wavy it was. His heart accelerated, and he drank his fill of her.

In that split second when the tire blew and the airbag hit his face, he'd wondered if he'd ever see her again. A strange silence had filled his head in those minutes. The horrific sounds faded to white noise as his head hit the roof. And he'd experienced a stillness, a peace. A clarity as the crash tossed his body from side to side.

But he'd felt sheltering arms. Infinite love. Someone who'd proven on Calvary He could be trusted. With everything.

Charlie's breath stopped as he and Evy stared at each other. The moment hung suspended. Stretching between them. Connecting them. Did she hate him? If she did, he deserved it.

She cleared her throat. "What is this I hear about you being a difficult patient, Deputy Pruitt?"

He gulped past the emotion lodged in his throat. "I'm not staying here."

She plucked his pants, the worse for wear, off a nearby chair. "Do you need help getting dressed?"

He narrowed his eyes. "No way I'm letting you dress me. Where's Jolene?"

"You've got control issues, Pruitt."

"You've got book issues, Shaw."

Evy laughed. He flushed. Then laughed, too.

"Stop." He clutched his rib cage. "Don't make me laugh. Sorry if I'm not up for the usual witty repartee we do so well."

Evy smiled. "We do banter well, don't we?"

In that instant, he recalled a brief flash of memory when the windshield shattered on impact. An image of him and Evy in the window seat of his house reading aloud a picture book with a small child between them. A dream? A vision? A prayer?

A lifeline.

She moved alongside the bed. "Does it hurt to talk? If so, I'll be quiet."

"That'll be the day." He shifted on the thin mattress and winced. "I don't mind talking. It's the breathing that hurts."

But that didn't matter, either. He was so deliriously glad to see her. In the parade of faithful friends, he'd wondered if she cared enough to come. Hoped she cared enough to come.

She did. If only a little.

Evy held up his pants. "Jolene can help you get dressed. But then I'm taking you home." She leaned over the bed. "And that's the way it's going to be, Charles Pruitt. Whether you like it or not."

"I like it."

He took a cautious exploratory breath. He

loved the intoxicating scent of her. Something exotic.

"Okay then." She opened the curtain. "Glad we understand each other."

He was a blessed man. In more ways than one. Why hadn't he seen that before?

Charlie didn't believe in luck. He believed in his training, his gut, in God's overarching orchestration of his life. And he believed in Evy.

He was tired of wrestling with doubt. Charlie was going to trust her. Without proof. As an act of faith. She didn't have anything to prove to him. Actually, it was the other way around. He was done with this so-called investigation of Honey's.

And he thanked God for the second chance to prove to Evy he was a man who could be trusted. With her secrets or not.

He'd be there for her—as long as she let him.

Chapter Eleven

An hour later, at his house, Charlie glanced at himself in the hall mirror. And shuddered. The air bag had saved his life. That plus the seat belt. And most of all, God. But the air bag hadn't done his face any favors.

Charlie fingered his chin, eyeing the abrasions and small cuts. Evy had helped him get in and out of her car. The journey from his driveway and up the porch steps had felt like climbing K2. He hated feeling helpless. So he fussed. She was too small to bear his hulking weight. She told him to shut up.

But she was stronger than she looked. The ballet training? Or the something she didn't want to talk about that had made her so strong on the inside?

She closed the front door with a decided click.

"Stop admiring yourself, Charlie, and sit down. Nothing has marred your handsomeness."

He shot her a look and grinned. The cut on his cheek burned. He told himself not to smile again. But it was hard not to smile when he was with Evy. "Glad to know you think I'm handsome."

She took his arm, leading him into the living room. "Not a news flash. It's common knowledge. And if I didn't already know you were handsome, all I had to do was ask you. You'd have told me, for sure."

He laughed. And immediately regretted it as he had to bend over double to cushion his ribs.

"Evy. Stop," he wheezed. "For pity's sake."

He glanced at the sofa. "If I go down now, I won't be able to get up."

She straightened his cockeyed collar. "What do you need?"

"Comfort food. But more than that, I want to take a shower." He planted his palms on her shoulders. "Don't attempt to *persuade* me otherwise…"

She sighed. "You peeked ahead two weeks to our reading of Jane Austen's *Persuasion*."

Charlie ran his hand behind the nape of her neck and tangled his fingers in her hair. "I like your hair this way. You should wear it loose more often."

Her lips twitched. "You've obviously been overmedicated."

"As a matter of fact, I like you, Evy Shaw. More than a lot."

"Suppose you get dizzy, fall down in the shower and split your head open on the tile?"

"Your over-the-top imagination rivals Catherine Morland's." He encircled her waist with his hands. "I'm suddenly feeling much better. But if worse comes to worst, you can give me mouth-to-mouth."

Evy rolled her eyes. "You wish, Deputy. I'm not the only one with an overactive imagination."

But she didn't move away. If anything, she settled in closer. Her head tucked into the hollow of his throat. Fitting, Charlie thought, just right in his arms.

Pieces of a puzzle coming together. Like God had made them to complete each other.

"My, my. You've been busy since book club last night. Reading ahead. Chasing bad guys. Surviving a near-death experience. When did you find time to sleep?"

"I didn't."

Her brow knitted. "Why not?"

"I couldn't sleep. I didn't like the way things ended between us. I'm sorry for being an idiot. I'll try to keep my idiocy under better control next time." He bit his lip and caught himself in an unconscious imitation of Evy. "If you'll give me a second chance."

"I'm sorry, too." She touched his lip with the tip of her finger. "Don't flip your car again. Okay?"

"Lesson learned." One glance at the staircase and he groaned. "Whose bright idea was it to put the bathrooms on the second floor?"

"I'll help you and then scrounge up something for you to eat."

His arm around her waist, she helped him tackle the stairs, one painful step at a time. At the landing, he stopped to catch his breath.

She frowned. "Maybe we should go back."

The afternoon sun spilled through the stained-glass window, a shimmer of blue, red and purple across her features. Bathing them in light.

He shook his head. "I'll take it from here."

She pushed her glasses to the bridge of her nose. "But Charlie—"

"I got this, Shaw. Stop hovering."

He seized the railing and hauled himself upward. He stole a look over his shoulder. She waited on the landing behind him, arms outstretched as if she aimed to catch him if he fell.

What she failed to realize, however, was that he'd already fallen. Hard. For her.

* * *

Evy didn't move until he made it to the top of the stairs. She held her breath, willing him to make it. He winked at her and disappeared inside the bathroom. She heard the squeak of a faucet, then the gushing torrent of water from the shower.

In the kitchen, she perused the contents of his pantry and rooted inside the cabinets for a skillet. She kept one ear cocked toward the ceiling, half afraid the next sound would be a thud.

But everything appeared normal as she scooped coffee grounds into the coffeemaker. As the fragrant aroma permeated the air, the faucet overhead creaked off. A few minutes later, a phone rang somewhere. The familiar *Bonanza* tune.

"Hey, Mom." His deep voice carried through the ceiling. "I'm fine. Really."

Evy mixed the batter. Turned on the range. Waited for the skillet to get hot and then poured in the mixture.

All of a sudden, she realized she hadn't detected any sounds of life from Charlie in a few minutes. Her pulse quickened. Was he okay?

"Evy!" he shouted from upstairs.

Leaving the skillet, she raced out of the kitchen to the bottom of the stairs. His hair still wet from the shower, Charlie stood on the landing. In a pair of gray sweatpants and wearing a much laundered maroon T-shirt.

She ran up the stairs, closing the distance between them. "What's wrong?"

He looked at his bare toes and up at her. "Could you help me the rest of the way? Please?"

She twined her arm around his waist. "Did you hurt yourself? Are you dizzy?"

He smelled good. Soap and the indefinable essence that was Charlie.

"No." He leaned into her. "I just missed you."

She let go of him. "You are so pathetic, Charles Pruitt. I ought to push you down the stairs myself for scaring me like that." But she feathered a lock of his hair off his forehead.

He captured her hand and brought it to his lips. She quivered. He looked way too appealing.

She'd always considered herself a woman of uncommon sense. But right now, sensibility warred with sense. And sensibility was winning.

Evy gulped. That T-shirt fit him so well. Did amazing things for his muscular build. It wouldn't do to tell him so. It would only inflate that already oversize ego of his. Squeezing his hand, she moved a safer distance away.

He smirked at her. With that lazy air of his as if he understood exactly what he was doing to her.

Charlie's face scrunched as he lifted his nose

in the air like one of Seth Duer's bird dogs. "Is that cinnamon I smell?"

"Oh, no." She skipped down the stairs. "It's going to burn."

Charlie followed at a slower pace. Fought through the pain. He forced his limbs to move despite the overwhelming urge to quit. Like he'd learned in his football days.

Don't give in. Never quit. Keep moving forward.

His aching muscles would thank him tomorrow. The more he moved now, the less stiff he'd be in the morning. Still, tell that to the pounding in his head.

When he walked into the kitchen, something stirred inside him at the sight of Evy flipping pancakes on the stove. He eased one hip onto the bar stool.

"Didn't know you could cook. I take my meals on the road. Hence my firsthand acquaintance with most of the restaurants in the area. And for the record, cops and doughnuts aren't an unfounded stereotype." He perked on the stool. "Is that coffee I smell?"

Evy snagged the coffeepot. "No thanks to you and your well-honed powers of distraction, but I managed to avoid burning the pancakes." She poured coffee into a blue ceramic mug. "Drink."

She pushed the mug across the granite island. "Jolene says I have to monitor you for signs of concussion. You're not allowed to sleep for twelve hours. So you're stuck with me inventing ways to keep you awake."

He wrapped his hand around the warmth of the mug. "That sounds promising."

"You should be so fortunate, Pruitt."

He silently agreed as he took a sip. "You make good coffee."

"Thanks. I wield a mean wok, too."

"Uh." He inched higher to inspect the contents of the frying pan. "That's not Chinese, is it?"

"No, although Mrs. Chan taught me everything I know."

Evy slid the spatula under the pancakes and plopped them into a stack on the plate. Squeezing a sandwich bag, she drizzled white glaze over the steaming pancakes.

She finished by making a smiley face with the icing. "There."

He dug his fork into the stack. "Fancy." He opened and closed his mouth around the bite. He chewed.

"Cinnamon-roll pancakes, my version of comfort food." She kneaded a dish towel with her hands. "I couldn't find any syrup. Mrs. Chan usually drizzled agave over mine."

"Don't need syrup. This is fabulous, Evy. Thank you."

She favored him with a sweet smile. "I'm glad you like it." She pivoted to the stove. "There's more if you're still hungry."

What he liked was seeing her in his house. So natural. So right it took his breath.

In marrying Honey, Sawyer Kole had done him the biggest favor of all time, Charlie belatedly realized. Leaving him available for when God brought a certain librarian into his life.

After he ate his fill—he insisted Evy eat something, too—he also insisted on helping her clean the kitchen.

"House rules. Whoever cooks, the other does the dishes."

"Really?"

"Yes, ma'am."

She gave him a fond look. "You Southern boys and your manners."

Propped against the sink, he rinsed off the plates. "We aim to impress."

As the afternoon became evening, it wasn't only his mother who called. His siblings called, too. At least, those not on an aircraft carrier. The phone nearly rang off the hook.

Reverend Parks. A slew of church ladies promising casseroles. Suppertime—and his prospects for home-cooked meals stretching into next week—was looking good.

After the last phone call, his shoulders drooped, and he decided to take a load off his feet by sitting on the sofa.

Evy gave him the once-over. "You've worn yourself out."

He leaned his head against the upholstery.

"Don't you dare close your eyes, Charles Pruitt."

His eyes flew open.

She wagged her finger. "You're not falling asleep on my watch."

His lips quirked. "Entertain me, then, Shaw."

She fiddled with the frame of her glasses and blushed.

He grinned. It never got old. Pushing Hula Girl's buttons.

She gave him an arched look.

He moistened his lips. "How about reading aloud the rest of *Northanger Abbey*? Don't want to get behind for book club."

She brightened. "I can do that."

Retrieving the book from the kitchen, she took the cushion next to his. She opened the book and found the bookmark where he'd stopped reading. At the end of every chapter, she asked him questions to make sure he was awake.

"You have the loveliest reading voice, Miss Shaw." He smiled. "Quite pleasing."

She eyed him over the top of her glasses, which had slid down on her cute little nose. She turned a page. "You are one of the good guys, Deputy Pruitt."

He pretended to polish his knuckle on his shirt. "What we have here, ladies and gentlemen, is a mutual admiration society."

She laid the book across her lap. "Could I ask you something?"

His lighthearted mood vanished. "You can ask me anything. You can trust me."

"I know I can trust you." She slipped off her shoes and tucked her legs under her. "Despite seeing you in the parking lot of the grocery store yesterday with Honey."

Charlie's gut twisted. What did she know? With that sharp brain of hers, what had she already guessed?

He feared how Evy would react to learning about what he'd done behind her back. "Go ahead and ask."

But what she asked wasn't what he expected.

"What happened between you and Honey Kole?" She smoothed her skirt over her knee. "If it's not too painful for you to tell me, I'd like to understand why she married Sawyer and not you." Evy dropped her eyes. "I know how much you love her." And she drew herself into a tight little ball. Shrinking into the pillow cushions.

He reached for her hand. "Stop that. Look at me."

Evy's eyes were a breathtaking blue behind her glasses.

"You don't need to do that. Not ever again. Not with me."

Her mouth trembled.

Charlie held on to her hand, refusing to let her slip away from him. Physically or emotionally. "For the record, I've come to realize over these last few weeks I never really loved Honey, not in the way you mean."

Evy sat so still, like she was holding her breath. He wished she would say something. When she didn't, he tried to put into words what he'd felt then and what he knew now.

"We dated in high school. Everyone, including me, figured we'd be married with the requisite two-point-five children."

Evy released his hand and put a throw pillow between them. "So you two were the golden boy and girl of the Eastern Shore, but things didn't work out as you'd planned."

He made a face. "I wouldn't call us golden…"

"Were you or were you not captain of the football team?"

He hunched his shoulders. "Well, yes."

She lifted her chin. "Both of you homecoming king and queen?"

"Yes," he grunted.

She pursed her lips. "You are a classic overachiever."

He cocked his head. "Said by a woman with multiple degrees who also speaks four languages, including English."

She shrugged. "Five, but who's counting?"

"I am." He stared at her. "What's the fifth?"

"Italian. Study abroad. Junior year." She fluttered her hand. "But let's get back to you."

He grimaced. "Let's not."

"Voted most likely to—"

"It's not the way you make it sound."

"Then tell me how it was." She crossed her arms around the pillow. "I don't mean to sound insensitive." She fretted at the pillow fringe. "I'm sorry she broke your heart, Charlie."

"Honey Duer may have hurt my pride. But I realize now, she never broke my heart."

From the skeptical look on her face, he could tell Evy wasn't sure she believed him. Fair enough. The last four years he'd *acted* as if Honey had broken his heart.

She tossed the pillow aside. "Then what's with you and Sawyer?" She inched close enough for Charlie to take hold of her hand again.

Charlie swallowed. "I admit it was hard to set

aside my pride. Especially in a place like Kiptohanock, where everyone had known us since we were kids. We were friends a long time. Before he came along."

"But what do you have against him?" Evy opened her hands, palms up. "He's a great guy."

"Did you learn nothing from Jane Austen, Evy? Appearances can be deceiving."

Her expression closed up. "Like how?"

Apparently steel wasn't a characteristic only of Southern magnolias.

"That first summer at the Kiptohanock Coast Guard station, everybody knew Sawyer Kole was trouble. He lived hard before he came to Kiptohanock. And he played hard, too. Drove Honey up and down the Shore in that flashy car he used to have. He was such a loser."

Evy went rigid. "That's not fair." She snatched her hand out of his grasp. "He's not a loser."

It galled Charlie how she always defended Sawyer.

"You weren't here, Evy. Seth Duer and her sister Amelia, were beside themselves." Charlie gritted his teeth. "And then, like the loser he is, he dumped her."

"Poetic justice for you." She glared. "His loss, your gain."

Charlie's teeth ached from clenching his jaw. He struggled to keep the vow he'd made after the accident. To give Evy space. And the benefit of the doubt.

But as his head pounded, he fought a losing battle to not interrogate her. To discover once and for all why she cared so much about Sawyer Kole.

"If you're implying I was glad he hurt Honey, you'd be wrong. But I was happy to see him reassigned off-Shore." Charlie glowered. "Before he dragged Honey into whatever sketchy hole he crawled out of."

Livid, Evy jumped off the couch. "What do you know about what he's had to overcome?" The pillow fell to the rug. "What would someone like you with your perfect, idyllic childhood know about someone like him?"

Charlie's mouth tightened. "What would you, Evy?" He struggled despite the pain to a more upright position.

She gestured at empty air. "No matter what you say about him, it's obvious he makes Honey happy. Her entire family loves him."

If anything was obvious after this conversation, it was how much Evy cared about Sawyer Kole. Charlie inhaled, waited for his pulse to steady.

With effort, using the armrest for support, he clambered to his feet. "That's now. The Duers say he's changed." Charlie wobbled, unsteady.

"When Kole returned, he rode to Honey's rescue in the middle of a hurricane. And the Duers forgave and forgot. I'm not sure I buy it." He squared his shoulders. "I sure haven't forgotten."

Evy stood toe-to-toe with Charlie. Not yielding an inch. Nor retreating from her unqualified devotion to Sawyer Kole.

"Why is it you find it so hard to trust, to believe the best in people? People can surprise you."

He scowled. "People surprise you all right. Every day. And not in pleasant ways."

"Why won't you believe people can change? Open your eyes, Charlie. See him, really see him, with those children. And with Honey."

"Open *your* eyes, Evy." He barely managed to avoid raising his voice. "What is it you think I do for a living? I don't rub shoulders on a daily basis with people at their best and brightest."

He raked his hand over his head and flinched when he lifted his arm. "Case in point."

"Let me get this straight." She somehow got in his face. All five-foot-three inches of her. "So if you never trust, then nobody can ever disappoint you again."

He cut his eyes at the ceiling. How had this become about him? "You got it."

Evy's mouth flattened. "Must get kind of lonely from that exalted position from which you view the rest of us less-than-perfect humans."

Charlie towered over her. "Why do you feel this completely undeserved and overwhelming need to defend Sawyer Kole's good name?"

He wanted to kiss her so badly. She, who wanted nothing from Charlie but friendship. Maybe after today, not even that.

The yearning in Charlie's heart intensified. "Why do you feel this bond with Kole?" He'd gone far beyond pride now. "You practically gush every time he talks to you."

Confusion darkened her eyes.

The ache deepened. "I saw you with Sawyer on the steps of the library yesterday. And I see how you look at him," he whispered.

"Oh no, Charlie." She took his hand in hers. Her skin felt so cool, so good against his. "You're wrong about me. And him."

How Charlie wanted to be wrong.

She let go of his hand. "I do love Sawyer."

The oxygen went out of his lungs. Her words cut worse than splinters of glass. Charlie staggered.

Evy caught hold of him. She cradled his cheek in her hand and bit back a sob. "He's my brother."

Chapter Twelve

Evy was relieved finally to tell her secret to Charlie. Somehow when she wasn't looking, Charlie Pruitt had sneaked past her defenses and taken residence in her heart.

He'd gone quiet at her news. She wasn't sure what to make of his silence. But Bernie and Dixie arrived, bringing dinner from Miss Jean, a friend of his mom's. The Ritz cracker chicken casserole was good. Evy thought she'd ask for the recipe.

With Bernie and Dixie putting the kitchen to rights, she told Charlie about Sawyer's offer to help her get over her fear of riding.

Charlie let out a breath. "I'm still trying to process everything you told me."

She bit her lip. "I can understand this must come as a shock."

Charlie cupped her cheek. "Will I see you tomorrow?"

She melted at his touch. "I'd like that." She pressed her lips into his palm.

His Adam's apple bobbed. Could it be she affected him the way he affected her?

"I'm still planning on doing story time tomorrow night after the library closes for the weekend. But I wanted no more secrets between you and me."

"Evy… I—" He swallowed.

She glanced at the mantel clock. "Hang in there, Deputy. It's almost time for another pain pill."

His gaze slid away.

The strain of the day must have caught up to him. Bernie and Dixie would have their hands full keeping him from nodding off.

He gestured toward the hall. "Would you help me?"

She eased him off the sofa and guided him into the study. Novel clutched under his arm, he headed straight for the window seat.

As she examined his battered features, her eyes misted. He'd come close—too close—to never sitting there again.

He raised his copy of *Northanger Abbey*. "Dixie's making me read the rest of the chapters out loud. She and Bernie are going to reenact the scenes." Charlie rolled his tongue in his cheek. "If that doesn't keep me awake, nothing will."

She laughed and, before she second-guessed herself, kissed his cheek. The hazel in his eyes deepened.

Evy ran her finger alongside the stubble sandpapering his jawline. "Don't have too much fun without me, Deputy. Remember those tender ribs."

He caught her hand. "Nothing is as fun without you."

"You've got good friends in your life, Charlie Pruitt."

"The best."

And he kissed her fingers. Her insides turned to liquid. The beat of her heart drummed in her chest.

"Oh, Evy," he sighed. "What in the world am I going to do about you?"

"Be well, Charlie. Till tomorrow."

She took a deep, steadying breath and walked out of his house while she still possessed the willpower to do so.

The next morning was cool and crisp. A harbinger of harvest season. She made a mental note to buy pumpkins to decorate the library porch.

When she reached the Keller farm, Sawyer

and several children had already gathered in the barn. The smell of hay and leather tickled her nose. Latasha hugged Evy.

Sawyer pushed back the brim of his hat. "Good morning." He smiled. "It's great to see you. I'm so glad you decided to join us."

Her pulse quickened. Would she ever get used to seeing him, having him even in a small way in her life again?

"It's good to see you, too."

For the next hour, she learned how to groom a horse and how to clean tack. Under his close supervision, she and the children brushed the horse's coat.

Latasha ran her hands through the horse's mane. "Alfalfa's hair is so pretty."

From over the horse's withers—Evy was inordinately proud she'd remembered that—Sawyer winked at Latasha. "Maybe sometime I can show you how to braid Alfalfa's mane."

He play-tugged one of the barrettes on Latasha's cornrows. "You two could match."

Blake, the not-so-holy terror of a succession of foster homes, made a face. "Alfalfa's a guy horse, Tash. Play beauty parlor on Darla."

Evy jutted her hip at Sawyer. "Tell me you didn't name the horses after the characters on *Little Rascals*?"

"That would've been Mr. Keller." Sawyer

laughed. "Not me. Before my time. I'm more of a *Star Trek* fan myself."

She blinked. "Really? Me, too. Original or *Next Generation*?"

"Original, for sure." Sawyer handed Latasha the curry comb. "But I liked *Next Generation* the best after that. *Voyager* third."

"Why *Star Trek*?"

Sawyer ran his hand over Alfalfa. "I liked the hope and optimism of brave new worlds. Of second chances."

He trained his eyes on the horse. "My sister and I used to watch the show together when my dad was…" He bit his lip.

Evy's breath hitched.

He shuffled his boots. "Afterward, no matter where I was, I kept watching. Made me feel connected to her." Uncomfortable with emotion, he moved away to oversee one of the kids.

Evy's heart pounded. She still had so many questions. Lifelong questions. But to probe further might open old wounds best left alone.

His back to the horse, Sawyer lifted one of the hooves and braced it between his legs. He showed them how to inspect and clean the hoof. Except for Blake, the children shied away, backing into Evy.

Latasha's eyes resembled large brown coins. "Are we going to have to do that?"

Sawyer shook his head. "Only if you want to. Thought I'd give you the complete picture of what we do to take care of our horse friends."

Blake stepped forward. "I'd like to learn." He tucked his thumbs in his belt and widened his hips.

A fair imitation of Sawyer's splayed-leg stance. A holdover from Sawyer's Coast Guard days? So many things she didn't know about Sawyer. So many things she'd probably never know.

Sawyer ruffled Blake's hair. "A man who boldly goes where no one has gone before. I like that. How about you, Evy?"

Evy smiled back. She'd done the right thing coming to Kiptohanock. She'd treasure these few memories forever.

Sawyer showed Blake how to touch Alfalfa's leg and pick up the hoof. Almost under the belly of the beast, Blake's grin was infectious. The other children admired his courage and told him so. Blake's posture broadened under their praise. His shoulders squared.

"I think that's enough for today." Sawyer ushered them out of the stall. "Next week, we'll tack Alfalfa, Darla and Spanky. Maybe somebody brave might want to do a short ride around the corral."

Blake tipped his pint-size cowboy hat with his

finger. Evy's heart turned over at the gesture so reminiscent of Sawyer. "I might be up for some of that action."

Sawyer nodded. "It's a plan, then." He secured the stall door. "Mr. Keller and Felicia have breakfast waiting in the kitchen. And I think I heard something about Long Johns, a personal favorite of mine." He laughed to himself as if at an inside joke.

A general stampede ensued as the children raced for the house.

"Don't forget to wash your hands," she called after them.

"You have a special gift with children, Evy," Sawyer said. "I wish you'd been around over the summer."

Evy wished so, too. But until she met Charlie, her efforts to infiltrate Keller's Kids Camp had been rebuffed. By Honey. Evy couldn't tell Sawyer that, though.

He gazed across the barnyard toward the white-framed farmhouse. "I think we've had a breakthrough with Blake. He's been such an angry, sullen kid." He ducked his head and brushed his hat against his thigh. "Been there. Been him."

Which told her a lot. About the time during their separation. About the years they'd missed knowing each other.

"Thanks for coming this morning, Evy."

She lifted her chin. "Thanks for inviting me. I'll be back tonight for story hour." She shrugged. "That's more my skill set."

He tapped his finger on the side of his nose. "Don't discount your equestrian talents."

"Very hidden equestrian talents."

He settled the hat on his head. "I'll make a proper rider out of you before we're done, I promise."

"I look forward to it." And she did.

At church the next day, she met Charlie's firefighter brother, Will. Older by a few years, but infinitely less handsome, Charlie assured her when he introduced them.

Will rolled his eyes. She laughed at the competitive yet close bond between the brothers. Like maybe she and Sawyer would've enjoyed if not for—

She decided not to go there. If wishes were horses, she'd be riding rainbows in the sky. What was done was done. She had now. And for now, that was enough.

"Where have you been hiding this lovely librarian, bro?" Will's eyes, the blue-green so many of the locals possessed, gleamed with mischief. "If I didn't live across the bay…"

Charlie arched his brow. "You may have forgotten that unlike you pretty boys lazing around the firehouse, I'm licensed to carry. And I'm not afraid to use it."

His brother laughed harder. "Evy, you look too smart to fall for the likes of this scoundrel."

Charlie's mouth twitched. She gave Will points for handling SuperDeputy. Poking good-natured fun in the way only a sibling could.

"Stick with me, sweetheart." Will elbowed his brother. "I'm the real reader in this family."

Charlie feigned outrage. "Absolutely untrue. Evy knows how I love a good book."

The rest of the week flew by for Evy. Will—to her regret and Charlie's alleged relief—went back home across the bridge.

She conducted the weekly after-school story time for the children of Kiptohanock. And of course, presided over the Thursday evening book club. To which Charlie, as usual, contributed his unique take on Austen literature.

After a week of enforced leisure, Charlie returned to work. They talked to each other or texted every day. He didn't push her to answer questions she was sure he must have. And she was grateful for his understanding.

Another Saturday came and went. She'd resisted Sawyer's efforts to get her into the saddle. Telling him she wanted the children to have first opportunity.

Those mornings were precious, a gift from God. The lessons wouldn't last forever, so she savored each one. As September rolled into October, she judiciously stayed out of Honey's way. Which wasn't as hard as she'd supposed.

Autumn on the Shore was a popular time for tourists to come for the fishing—who knew?—and for couples seeking a romantic getaway. With the help of her dad, Honey kept busy running the inn. Which was fine by Evy.

Less drama. Less tension. A win-win for everyone.

During Saturday night storytelling at Keller's, she could see Charlie observing Sawyer from a distance. Imagination or wishful thinking, but perhaps with a tad less censure? She prayed for both of them. As Sawyer shared more of his personal story with the children each week, Charlie's attitude softened toward her brother.

When Charlie wasn't on duty, they met for dinner most nights. For Chinese or over takeout at his house. He was fast becoming her best friend.

She wished she could capture each moment with Charlie and Sawyer. Hold them forever. But the days were getting shorter. In more ways than one.

One evening, she and Charlie met by the Kiptohanock seawall. She felt the rosy heat of the sunset through the fabric on the back of her cardigan as they gazed across the harbor toward the barrier islands. The twilight deepened.

"Why haven't you told Sawyer that you're his sister?"

She'd been waiting for Charlie to ask the obvious question. The sun hung suspended one moment more before disappearing beyond the line of the horizon. She turned away from the boats bobbing in the marina and faced him.

"My brother has a life here. A good life without me. I don't want to spoil that for him. To create unrealistic obligations he can never fulfill."

"Why do you think you'd spoil his life, Evy?"

Her eyes flitted to where the white church steeple pierced the indigo-streaked sky. The peace of the evening enveloped her. "There's no place for me in his life, Charlie. You know it's true. For whatever reason, his wife hates me."

A muscle jumped in Charlie's cheek.

"She'll never willingly let me into the circle of his life. I'd always be the outsider. He has a family now. A family who loves him. I refuse to disrupt that. He doesn't need me."

"You don't know what he needs. The things he's said to the kids…" Charlie shook his head. "I'm starting to believe Sawyer never stopped looking for you. Being in his life could bring the closure you both need. And also the beginning of a long-awaited chapter."

"I can't take that risk." Her voice grew small. "Suppose he wouldn't be happy to know who I am?"

The wind blew a wisp of her hair across her cheek. Before she could brush it back, Charlie's fingers did it for her. She'd taken to wearing it loose when she was with him. He seemed to enjoy watching her hair play across her shoulders.

"I hate it when you sell yourself short, Evy Shaw. I can't imagine anyone not being happy to know you."

She trembled. "Are you happy to know me, Charlie?"

He tilted her chin upward. "Let me show you how happy." Bending, his lips claimed hers.

Evy's knees nearly buckled. But he held her in a tight grip against his chest. His mouth on hers was gentle. Their first real kiss.

Joy rocketed through her being. She swayed. He tasted like sweet tea.

Her fingers spread against his shirt, she felt the pounding of his heart beneath her hand. After a moment he pulled away so they could both regain their breath.

"That happy enough for you, Evy?" His voice was a husky whisper.

She liked being held in the circle of his arms. She didn't know the last time she'd felt so safe. So cared for. So loved?

Her mouth went dry. Was it possible for someone like Charlie to love someone as insignificant as her?

With surprising intensity, she believed that God had brought them together. In her quest to find her brother, God had also provided much more than she could've ever possibly imagined.

"I'm glad I told you my secret, Charlie. I was afraid at first, but I don't want there to be any secrets between us."

Like a bucket of ice water in the face, Charlie flinched. He needed to tell Evy the truth. He made an excuse about needing to get some shut-eye. But in reality, he couldn't stomach his own deceit any longer.

All the more reason why he should've come clean with Evy then and there. But he hadn't. He'd stalled. Rationalizing as he headed past the square toward home that he needed more time. To think through how best to phrase his complicity in the conspiracy against her.

Like there was a good way to say, "Oh, by the way, Evy. I joined the book club and pretended to be your friend so I could spy on you because an old, not-so-good friend asked me to betray you."

That was going to go over well. Though he hadn't pretended long. When she looked at him with those big blue eyes of hers behind the horn-rimmed glasses...her eyes full of him...?

Upon reflection of Evy's winsome ways, the pretense probably hadn't survived that first dinner over Chinese. 'Cause Evy and even the hen party book club were the first things he thought about in the morning. And the last at night.

Evy Shaw had made a reader out of him. Go figure. And a believer, too. A believer in a second-chance God and in second-chance love.

So why was he finding it so hard to tell the truth? Tossing and turning on his mattress, he punched his pillow.

Because he was terrified that if he told Evy the actual circumstances and motivation surrounding their friendship, she'd lose her faith in him. He'd lose any chance for something more. Something real.

Though how real any relationship could be founded upon lies, he didn't want to consider.

Pride? Oh, yeah. For sure.

He scrubbed his hand over his face. Telling her the truth would only hurt Evy. Maybe she didn't ever need to learn the truth. Not when the truth now was that he cared deeply for her.

As more than just a friend. She'd found her brother. She loved her job. She had good friends like Dixie and one for the record books, Mrs. Davenport. She'd finally found a home, a place to belong, in Kiptohanock.

Viewed in that light, he was doing Evy a favor by not telling her the whole truth.

The past was the past. And the past was where the past should stay. Evy herself had said that. There was no good reason for her to learn about his secret involvement.

His conscience smote him. No good reason, except it was the truth. He ought to call Evy right now and explain. She was a forgiving person. She'd understand.

Charlie reached for his cell lying on the nightstand. He let his hand drop. He glanced at the digital clock. It was so late. Too late? Maybe tomorrow he'd call. Maybe… He was a coward and he knew it.

And instead of calling Evy, he texted Honey.

In no uncertain terms, calling off his part in the investigation. It was the best he could do for now.

Until he worked up the courage to face Evy's rightly deserved scorn.

Chapter Thirteen

Saturday morning, Evy faced her fear and got on the horse.

Her shoulders tense, she gripped the reins. "It's awfully high off the ground…"

Latasha climbed onto the corral gate. "You look good up there, Miss Evy."

Without thinking, Evy let go of the reins to push her glasses farther up the bridge of her nose. The horse sidestepped. With a quick intake of breath, she grabbed the reins again.

"Try to relax." Sawyer stroked the horse's head. "I'm going to lead you around the corral." He took hold of the lead rope, and the horse moved forward.

Going rigid, she fought the urge to scream. Only just remembering she was supposed to set an example for the children. Sawyer probably believed she was the biggest ninny who'd ever lived.

She blinked away the moisture in her eyes. Why was she such a coward? Good for nothing but books. Her posture stiff, she clung to the reins as Sawyer led the horse around the corral.

Blake straddled the fence railing. "At first, I was scared, too," he called. "Like the day I went to my first foster home. But it wasn't as bad as I thought it'd be."

Sawyer shot a look over his shoulder at Evy. That admission from Blake was huge.

Evy swallowed against her fear. "Any advice, Blake?"

"Go with the flow." Blake lifted his chin. "Don't fight the sway. Adjust your body to the horse."

Sawyer smiled as they plodded past the boy. "I couldn't have said it better myself."

Under his child-sized Stetson, Blake's eyes shone with pride. The good kind of pride. And schooling herself to follow his advice, she loosened her stranglehold on the reins. She inhaled and exhaled to steady her nerves.

"Take your gaze off the ground. Keep your eyes fixed on the direction you want to go." Sawyer's breath made puffs in the frost-tinged October air. "The horse will follow your lead."

She fixed her eyes on rounding the circuit of the corral. "Good advice for life."

He threw her a grin. "I guess it is. Never thought of it that way before."

She forced her body to imitate the horse's rocking motion. She took her eyes off how far she could fall and instead focused on the view from her lofty perch. She scanned the ring of children who'd become so dear to her.

Her gaze flickered toward the hip-roofed barn. Past the pastures and fence line. To the flume of dust beneath the wheels of an incoming vehicle. She admired the farmhouse across the barnyard. And the glorious red-and-yellow tapestry of the trees.

Latasha clapped her hands together. "You're doing it, Miss Evy!"

Blake waved his hat in the air. "Ride 'em, cowgirl."

She laughed until she noticed Sawyer had let go of the lead. He leaned against a post, arms crossed across his denim jacket, a proud smile on his face.

"Wait—" She half turned in the saddle as the horse plodded by. "If you're not—then—oh, no—I can't ride by myself…" Her heart leaped into her throat.

"Too late." Sawyer gave her a crooked smile. "You *are* riding by yourself."

"B-but..." The horse slogged forward. A car door slammed.

"Like learning to ride a bike." He nudged his hat higher on his forehead. "At some point, the training wheels have to come off."

"Easy for you to say," she huffed and held on for dear life. "You ever try learning to ride a bike in San Francisco?" She clenched her jaw. "Let me tell you, mister. It's one giant whoosh downhill. Next stop, Japan." The horse lumbered on. "S-Sawyer..."

"Breathe, Evy. You're doing great."

She sucked in a breath at the strange sensation of her name on his lips. Something wasn't right about Sawyer calling her Evy. But the name he used to call her eluded Evy.

The horse completed its circle around the corral and stopped beside Sawyer. Her eyes cut to Sawyer. The horse whinnied.

She'd done it. She'd really done it. Ridden a horse all by herself.

"I did it," she whispered.

He cocked his head. "I have a feeling anything you set your mind to do, you do."

Giddy with accomplishment, she soaked in his approval.

"We'll have you cantering around the meadow before you know it."

"Quite the man of faith, aren't you?"

He grinned. "Practice makes perfect."

She returned his grin. Who'd have thought? Evy Shaw, a horse-riding librarian. She straightened her shoulders.

Taking hold of the bridle, he led Evy to the gate. "That's enough for today. Don't want to overdo it. I have a feeling tomorrow morning you won't thank me for the aching muscles you never knew you had."

He tied off the rope and reached for her. Hands planted on her waist, he swung Evy off the horse. She eased to the ground.

"Great job, Evy."

Her legs felt like mush. She held on to his forearm to get her bearings as the earth tilted for a second.

"Give yourself a minute to recover your land legs."

"Like getting off a boat?"

"Exactly."

She heaved a sigh of relief. "It wasn't as bad as I thought."

"Now there's a ringing endorsement of my training skills."

"I didn't mean—" She flushed and glanced up.

His light blue eyes twinkled. He was teasing her. Like he used to.

A palpable memory shot through Evy so

quickly she almost failed to capture it. Of a much younger Sawyer and her towheaded self as a child. A grimy sofa. A television screen.

She gasped at the clarity of the image. Her lips parted. She quivered from head to toe.

And something flickered across Sawyer's face, too. He dropped his hands. Staggered.

Chest heaving, his eyes darted, looking everywhere but at Evy. He scrubbed the back of his neck. "Who's next? Latasha? Blake? Rayna?"

Hands shot into the air. "Me."

"Me."

"Me."

He moved toward the children. And when he did, Evy got a clear view of the driveway. Where Honey Kole stood motionless at the edge of the barn.

Evy took a step toward Honey, but Honey headed toward the cabins. That moment between Evy and Sawyer—Honey could have easily gotten the wrong idea. A mistaken impression.

She hurried after Honey, who despite her advanced state of pregnancy gave the shorter-limbed Evy a run for her money to catch up. "Honey, wait..." She followed Honey inside the girls' cabin.

Honey busied herself straightening the bunk

beds. "Why are you always here playing at being Sawyer's new best buddy?"

Evy closed the cabin door behind her in case the children heard voices and came looking for her or Honey.

Honey crossed her arms. "Why can't you leave my family alone?"

"Sawyer was trying to help me get over my fear of horses for the children's sake."

"The children?" Honey's eyes blazed. "How dare you use those innocent children in whatever game you're playing." She laid her hand over her abdomen. "This is my life. My life and Sawyer's."

"You have it wrong."

"I don't think so." Honey's face contorted as if she were fighting tears. "From the minute you set foot in Kiptohanock, you've done nothing but insinuate yourself in my family's business." Honey's mouth twisted. "You may have temporarily beguiled Charlie Pruitt with your four-eyed, high-heeled little-girl-lost routine, but I see right through you to the manipulative—"

"Manipulative?" Voice rising, Evy planted her hands on her hips. "You want to talk about manipulative, Honey Duer? What about what happened between you and Charlie? How you strung him along between Sawyer's Shore assignments?"

"How dare you? You know nothing about me or my relationship with Charlie or with my husband, either." She jutted her chin. "And it's Honey *Kole*."

"I know plenty," Evy sneered. "I'm sick of girls like you. The helpless Southern belle when it suits you. The iron hand in the not-so-velvet glove when it doesn't."

"There's no room in my life or Sawyer's for someone like you."

Evy curled her lip. "You may be the most self-serving, selfish human being I've ever met in my life. What a good guy like Sawyer sees in you is beyond my comprehension."

Honey's nostrils flared. "I've tried—God knows I've tried—to tolerate you for the sake of the children. But coexistence is no longer an option. I'm sick and tired of 'why can't we be friends and get along,' Evy Shaw." Honey's brows furrowed into a V. "If that's even your real name."

"It's my name."

Evy frowned. Wasn't it? The only one she had, anyway.

"Get out," Honey jabbed her finger at the door. "Get out of this program. Get out of my life. No one wants you here."

Evy choked at her words.

And something rose in Evy. Something she

wouldn't have believed was there. Like a smoldering ember bursting into flame.

Snatching one of the pillows from a bunk bed, she threw it at Honey's head.

Evy almost laughed at the wide-eyed disbelief in Honey's eyes. Then it registered what she'd done. She'd thrown a pillow at a pregnant woman.

Honey grabbed the pillow and threw it at Evy. It bounced to the rug. Evy retrieved it as Honey yanked another pillow off a bed. "I won't let you hurt my family."

Pillow held high, Honey came at Evy from across the room like some blue-painted Scot from *Braveheart*. Evy blocked Honey's downward arc with an upward sweep of her own pillow.

"Take that!" Honey yelled.

With a whack—the pillows collided. Parrying and thrusting. Tit for tat. Careful to keep contact away from the baby, she and Honey jousted around the cabin.

"You take that," Evy shouted.

Honey slammed her pillow on top of Evy's head. The seam split. Feathers erupted.

Evy sputtered and blew a feather away from her nose. She thwacked Honey on the head. Duck feathers flew around the room.

Settling on the beds and on the rugs. Resting on Honey's shoulders. Covering Evy's head.

Honey collapsed against the bed with laughter. "You look like a molted bird."

Evy laughed. "You ought to look at yourself."

The door to the cabin creaked open.

"What's all the racket in here?" Sawyer poked his head inside.

Covered in the white down of the feathers and still laughing, Evy pivoted.

The color drained from his face. His gaze shifted from Evy's hair to her face. And his blue eyes went opaque.

"Cotton?"

Her heart thundered. A thread of memory wove through her mind.

"Is it really you?" His voice trembled. "My little sister?"

He raked an unsteady hand over his head, dislodging his hat. It fell to the ground. He didn't notice. Behind him on the cabin stoop, Charlie peered over Sawyer's shoulder.

Sawyer fell against the doorframe. "My baby sister?"

With her heart too full to speak, Evy nodded.

Honey made a muted sound. She covered her mouth with her hand. "Oh, no. Oh, no."

In one stride, Sawyer crossed into the cabin

and gathered Evy into his arms. "After all this time...thank You, Lord."

He hugged her as if he'd never let go.

"We've found one another, Cotton. At last."

"Your name is Evangeline?" Sawyer shook his head. "No wonder I couldn't find you." His eyes watered. "I searched for such a long time."

Charlie watched the play of emotion across Evy's face. The tremulous unfolding of joy. Like a rose opening to the warmth of sunlight.

Sawyer sat beside Evy on one of the bunk beds. A tear trekked down his cheek. "Your name was Jane. Jane Kole. Why did they change your given name?"

Evy gazed at Sawyer through her tears. "My adopted mother decided my name was too plain."

She gave a brittle laugh, which hurt Charlie in a deep place inside himself. "Too plain-Jane. Literally. So she renamed me Evangeline. After the poem by Longfellow." Evy shrugged. "As she's such a renowned literature scholar, I've always been grateful it wasn't something like Hortensia."

Jane.

Charlie wondered if Evy consciously connected her fascination with Jane Austen to her real self. An attempt to keep close to her real identity? Maybe a way of surviving emotionally through the pages of the novels Jane Austen penned so long ago. A link to who she'd once been—still was—in the secret places of her soul.

Obviously intelligent, how did her parents not grasp what they'd done to her? Severing Evy not only from her brother but also from her truest self. Forcing Evy to feel inadequate. Making her believe the only way she could belong to them was by making Jane Kole disappear.

Adding to the undeserved guilt she'd carried all these years. For being the lucky one to be adopted. About that, Charlie wasn't so sure. Anger surged through him.

Silent witness to the long-awaited reunion between brother and sister, Charlie seized a broom to clean up the mess on the cabin floor. Honey remained frozen next to the braided rug.

He shuddered inside, thinking of the mess still awaiting cleanup once Sawyer and Evy learned what he and Honey had done. The part they'd played in nearly preventing Sawyer from ever finding his sister.

"I looked for you, too, Sawyer. I remembered only bits and pieces from before. But I found some papers the day I graduated from Stanford. They led me to Oklahoma for my graduate degree."

Evy's mouth drooped. "But you'd joined the Coast Guard. As soon as I'd get a new lead on your location and follow, you'd already moved on. I was afraid I'd never find you. Or know you. Until the library job opened up here in Kiptohanock."

"You were five, Jane. I mean, Evy. Only five when Child Protective Services took us away from the rental house where our mother..."

Sawyer took a ragged breath . "At first we were together. A few weeks. But then—" He ground his jaw. Evy inserted her smaller hand in his work-roughened one.

Honey flinched. Charlie watched her gaze flit from Sawyer to Evy and back again. She was shaking harder than Evy. Unraveling before his eyes. Shocked beyond words. A rarity in his considerable experience with Honey.

"I was placed with Bradford and Ursula Shaw when they were instructors at the university in Oklahoma."

Sawyer nodded. "I met them. The social worker cautioned me to remain quiet. But when they saw you—" His grip tightened on Evy. "They only had eyes for you, Jane. Remarking how pretty they thought your blond hair was."

"That's why you called me Cotton. I didn't remember until just now."

"It became clear they only wanted you." A

bleak expression filled his eyes. "I can't blame them. I was an angry preteen. I'd given the emergency foster parents nothing but trouble in trying to stay close to you. I was more than the Shaws were willing to take on."

Evy worried her lower lip between her teeth. "I'm sorry, Sawyer. Sorry they didn't choose you, too."

His features softened. "Don't be. You were their princess in a tower."

Evy sighed. "In the end, I think I was also more than they bargained for. They had so little understanding of children. Especially a child like me with big gaping holes in her heart."

Sawyer put his arm around Evy's shoulders. "I'd hoped—prayed before I even understood what prayer was about—that you'd be loved and taken care of. Cherished."

"They weren't bad people, Sawyer. In their own way, they were good to me. They kept me safe. They fed and educated me. Gave me everything except what I wanted most—my brother."

Honey slipped away. As superfluous to the reunion between brother and sister as Charlie.

Evy swallowed. "I soon learned to stop asking for you. It upset them."

"I'm sorry, Cotton."

"We don't have to be sorry anymore. God has brought us together. In His time and in His way." She squeezed his hand. "And I for one am so thankful."

For the first time, Sawyer changed his focus to Charlie. "You knew?"

Charlie shrugged. "Only for a few weeks."

"You've been a good friend to my sister. I appreciate you looking after her."

Charlie winced. Not as good a friend as he should have been. Once Sawyer and Evy learned the truth, would either of them ever speak to him again?

Now was the moment to tell the truth. But this secret involved Honey. He couldn't throw her under the bus. Not without allowing her to break the news to her husband in her own way.

And then he had a tempting thought. Perhaps she'd never tell Sawyer. Perhaps the truth of their interference need never come to light.

It would serve no purpose except to hurt Evy and Sawyer. They'd found each other against all odds. Now was not the time to cause trouble. There was no good reason to come clean. Not now that the truth was out in the open.

The truth.

Wasn't keeping silent the most loving thing Charlie or Honey could do? What good would come from clouding the real issue—that a brother and sister had been reunited at long last? But his conscience warred within him.

He'd been raised to do the right thing. To value honesty above everything else. To live with integrity. The truth would set Charlie free of the lies and the insidious doubts.

But the truth could also destroy his relationship with Evy. Was he willing to risk that?

"I don't remember much of that time before, Sawyer." Evy's voice grew softer. "But I do remember how you always took the beating our father meant for me when he was—" She choked off a sob, and her brother gathered her in his arms.

At the picture her words painted, Charlie's heart twisted. Just thinking about her father laying hands on sweet little girl Evy made him ache inside. Charlie's parents were wonderful. But suppose as children he or his brothers had had to stand between an abusive parent and their sister, Anna, for instance? New respect grew within Charlie for the courage of the younger Sawyer Kole. And gratitude for saving Evy, despite everything else, from at least those kinds of scars.

When the siblings began sharing bittersweet glimpses of lonely childhoods, he left the cabin. He justified his decision by reasoning it would be better to allow Sawyer and Evy a chance to get to know each other again before casting a stone in tranquil waters.

Better, though, for whom?

Chapter Fourteen

That night, Sawyer led a combined story time with the boys and the girls by the bonfire in the meadow. From Evy's perspective, he seemed lighter. More at ease within his own skin.

And blessed beyond words, she marveled at the goodness of a God who'd given Evy back her brother. The only person alive who knew her before. Before she was Evy.

Before she was a librarian. When she was just Jane. Cotton-headed Jane.

And places long raw inside herself were assuaged. Like the balm in Gilead she'd heard about in church. Soothing wounded souls.

Questions she'd been afraid to ask were answered. As for the other empty places she'd attempted to fill with her books, God was doing work there, as well. For that, she felt a tremendous awe that somebody would do that for her. And she also felt an immense gratitude.

In the glow of the bonfire, Sawyer read the children another story. About a father who wasn't good to his children. About all the things a boy wished his father would do. About the boy who decided to grow up to be the father he wished he'd had.

Sawyer's gaze cut across the flames to Honey. Her hand rested atop her belly over their child. He teared up. As did Evy, and yes, even Mr. Keller. Honey, however, kept her gaze on the ground.

As for SuperDeputy Charlie? Since her unexpected reunion that morning, she'd not had the chance to talk to him. If she was at the corral with Sawyer, Charlie seemed to be needed on the boat with Felicia and Mr. Keller. While Evy served lunch, Charlie prepped for crafts.

A sliver of doubt inched its way into her otherwise perfect evening. Was Charlie avoiding her? But unable to think of any good reason why he should, she dismissed the discomfiting thought.

Their time would come. Charlie had been the best kind of friend these last few months. The best, truest friend she'd ever had. Standing by her side while she went through this experience.

Today was probably about Charlie giving her and Sawyer space to get reacquainted.

After the children went home Sunday afternoon, she'd make sure Charlie understood how much she appreciated his unconditional support. A smile played around her lips.

Maybe dinner over wonton soup and egg rolls. Followed by some light reading in that window seat of his... Her toes curled in her Keds just thinking about it.

As sparks drifted upward, blinking and vanishing against the blue velvet night sky, her attention drifted to Honey. Standing alone outside the light cast by the fire. In the shadows.

Evy didn't like how things had ended between them when Sawyer stumbled upon the truth. She and Honey needed to talk. She needed to apologize again for causing Honey to worry. They needed to come together for Sawyer's sake. For the sake of family.

Family. Her family and Sawyer's. It was important that she and Honey go forth with no more misunderstandings between them. For Sawyer's sake. For the future.

Evy exhaled. So many wonderful and mixed up feelings all at the same time. Knees pulled to her chin, she basked in the warmth of the fire on this chilly October night. At the thought of a future full of bright possibilities. For instance, she'd be an aunt.

She almost laughed aloud. An aunt. She vowed she'd be the best aunt in the world.

Evy smiled thinking of celebrating a real Eastern Shore Thanksgiving this year. At Christmas, foil-wrapped gifts around a tree. If she had to guess, she'd guess no artificial, frosted trees for Kiptohanock homes. The Duers and Pruitts probably cut their trees from the woods.

She gave a happy sigh. Easter egg hunts. Birthday parties. Building castles on the sandy beach of a barrier island next summer. She felt dizzy with delight. Exhilarated. Happier than she'd ever been.

She never could've imagined the good gifts God had placed within her reach. God was so good. She wasn't sure she'd be able to sleep tonight. Everything had changed for her today. Love had changed everything for Evy.

Because love—her breath caught—love always changed everything.

It was the final night of the final weekend of foster camp. So Evy closed their time together with a particular favorite of hers—*Goodbye*. The book was about how sometimes family had to live in different homes, but that didn't mean goodbye forever. Just goodbye for now.

Looking back over the last few months, Evy

reflected on the privilege of taking part in Sawyer's foster kid ministry. The blessing she'd received by sharing in the lives of children like Latasha, Rayna and Blake far outweighed anything she'd done for them.

It was late when she left the farm. With her relationship restored with her brother, she hoped to see the children again next summer. She'd not dared dream of staying in Kiptohanock until today. And she lay awake pondering how she could forge a new relationship with her sister-in-law, too.

The next afternoon, Evy passed the van driven by Mr. Keller with Felicia and the children returning to their foster families. They spotted Evy in her car, and a flurry of waving erupted from inside the van.

Anxious to make amends, she parked beside Sawyer's truck in the yard. And arrived to the sound of angry, raised voices coming from the barn. In the middle of a heated argument, Honey and Sawyer faced each other on opposite sides of the barn.

Evy was preparing to tiptoe away—when she heard her name.

"I can't believe you'd do that, Honey. To me. To my sister, Evy." He took off his hat and flung it into the dust. "How dare you! That's outlandish even for you."

Evy hung back in the shadows. What had Honey done?

"But I didn't know she was your sister." Honey closed the distance between herself and Sawyer. "I believed I was protecting you." She seized hold of his denim-clad arm.

He shook off Honey's restraining hand. "You were protecting yourself." He started for the other end of the open barn.

"Where're you going?" Tears rolled down Honey's cheeks. "Please, let me explain."

Sawyer didn't break stride. "I can't talk to you about this. Not when I might say something I'd regret. I've got fence wire to restring."

"Please, Sawyer…" Honey reached in his direction. Her hand dropped to her side.

Evy was devastated at what she'd witnessed. This was her fault. Honey and Sawyer were at odds. Because of her.

She backtracked to her car. This was exactly what she'd feared. She'd never wanted this. She crawled inside her vehicle.

The glowing future she'd dared to envision for herself and Sawyer over the last twelve hours dissipated like morning mist over the tidal marsh.

Resting her forehead against the steering wheel, she sobbed for what her coming to town had cost all of them. Her worst fears had come true.

Somehow she had to make things right between Honey and Sawyer. Unearthing a tissue in the glove compartment, she wiped her eyes and went in search of Honey.

Evy found Honey on the ridge overlooking the creek, which meandered out to sea. "I'm sorry, Honey."

"What're you apologizing for?" Honey stared over the water. "For not telling us sooner?" Shoulder muscles taut, she cradled her hands over her protruding stomach. "For telling us at all?"

Maybe she was apologizing for existing. And Evy understood then that, despite all the wishing in the world, she and Honey would never be friends. As she'd once predicted, each piece of Sawyer's life would be jealously guarded by Honey and shared with Evy only with reluctance.

And Evy couldn't—wouldn't—put Sawyer in that difficult position between his wife and his sister.

Yet something inside Evy refused to be sorry that at last she and Sawyer had met again. They'd had yesterday together to be brother and sister, if only that once.

She let the breath trickle from between her lips. "I'm sorry I ruined everything."

Honey jerked around. "What?"

"If I hadn't come here…" Evy chewed at her lower lip.

"Sawyer once said the same thing to me," Honey whispered. "About ruining everything he touched." She shook her head. "It wasn't true."

Honey's brown eyes took on a fierce glow. "I told him to never say it again." She lifted her chin. "And he hasn't. Because of me and my dad and what everyone in Kiptohanock has helped him see about himself."

"I'm glad he has you and your family. I should've stayed away." Evy fought to control the tremor in her voice. "I've never brought anyone anything but trouble. I'm so very sorry, Honey, more than I can say, for spoiling everything."

Honey's brows drew together in a frown. "What kind of place did the two of you come from that you both grew up feeling like that?" She closed her eyes. "What kind of people do that to children?"

When she opened her eyes, Evy was startled by the moisture welling in Honey's brown eyes. And remorse. "No, Evy. I should be the one apologizing to you. I'm no better than them for making you feel like that. You haven't ruined anything." Honey's lips quivered. "I'm always a little slow on the uptake. I don't deal well with change. We each battle our own wounds. Our own insecurities."

"Wounds? You?" Evy fingered the frame of her glasses. "Delmarva's Hostess with the Mostest? Kiptohanock's sweetheart?"

"All of us have hurt places inside us that scar over but never completely go away, Evy." Honey rubbed her forehead. "Someday I'll tell you about my losses. About my mom and Caroline, who only came home to us last spring."

"Someday?"

Honey's gaze bored into Evy. "We're family now. You, me, Sawyer and Baby Kole." She made an expansive gesture. "And you haven't really lived, Evy Shaw, until you've lived through a Duer family Thanksgiving."

Evy's heartbeat elevated. Was she hearing Honey right? "You'd want me to stay here? In Sawyer's life?"

Honey touched Evy's arm. "Family sticks together. You and Sawyer have a lifetime of catching up to do."

"But—"

"You don't spoil things, Evy." Honey's voice hitched. "You've brought such peace and closure to his life already. And I love him too much to keep that from him."

Evy took a quavery breath.

"Would you forgive me for the last few

months?" Honey swallowed. "Would you give me a second chance? I'd like for us to get to know one another, too. To find our way to friendship."

"You and me?"

"We can't be that different if Sawyer loves us both." Honey smiled. "And the fact that we both love him so much gives us the greatest common ground of all, don't you think?"

"But what about the problems I've caused between you and Sawyer?"

"Trust me, when you know Sawyer Kole the way I know Sawyer Kole, he blows hot but he doesn't stay mad long." She cut her eyes at Evy. "He's had a lot of practice forgiving me. Would you forgive me?" Honey extended her hand. "I'd love for us to start over." Honey squared her shoulders. "Hello, my name is Honey Kole, and I'm so pleased to meet you, Evy Jane Shaw." Her cheeks lifted. "Sawyer's beloved little sister, Cotton."

Tears burned Evy's eyelids as she took Honey's hand. "If you're sure you want me to stay, I will."

Honey squeezed Evy's hand. "I'm sure."

"Okay." Evy lifted her chin. "Hello, my name is Evy—" she moistened her lips "—Evy Jane Shaw, and I'm so pleased to meet you, Honey

Duer Kole." She smiled through her tears. "Sawyer's beloved Kiptohanock sweetheart."

Then they embraced.

Dashing tears from her eyes, Honey broke away first. "Sorry, but I need to sit down." She put a hand to the small of her back. "This standing is killing me."

Evy held her arm. "Let's go find Sawyer."

Honey nodded. "About that ruined business, though?"

Evy cocked her head.

A mischievous smile lit Honey's face. "If you'd never come to Kiptohanock, it's no secret that one particular deputy sheriff's life would've definitely been deprived of knowing you."

"You think he feels that way?" Evy bit her lip. "Really?"

"Trust me. One female to another. I know these things." Honey slipped her arm around Evy's shoulders. "This is going to be great. I always wanted to pass the Youngest Sister baton to someone else." Honey gave Evy a sly sideways look. "And guess what, little sis? Tag, you're it."

But her laughter changed into a groan. Honey's face went white. She clutched her belly.

Evy gripped Honey's arm. "What's wrong?"

Sucking in a breath, Honey's eyes darted to her feet. "My water." She gasped. "It just broke."

* * *

Hammer raised, Sawyer fisted his other hand. "I ought to punch you in the face, Charlie Pruitt."

The ex-Coastie radiated with anger. Bareheaded, his short blond hair—a darker version of Evy's—stood up on end as if he'd been raking his hands through it.

Close to the end of Charlie's shift, Honey's text had brought him to the farm posthaste. Warning him that she'd told Sawyer about what she and Charlie had done. Charlie was ashamed of what they'd done.

The dishonesty. The conspiracy against Evy. The disloyalty.

He hurried over to the farm only to spot several vehicles, including Evy's Mini Cooper, but no one in sight.

Charlie found Sawyer along the fence line. Pounding the barbed wire in place like he wished it was Charlie's head. And he didn't blame Sawyer for his reaction. This man wielding a hammer was Evy's only true family.

"I deserve a pounding," Charlie said. "And worse."

He and Sawyer had formed an uneasy truce over the last month. Broken now by Charlie's duplicity.

"You'd like that, wouldn't you? To provoke me

into taking a swing at you. So you can charge me with assaulting a police officer."

"This has nothing to do with me being a deputy."

Charlie removed the badge pinned to his uniform and stuck it inside his pocket. "This is you being Evy's brother. And me, deserving to be knocked flat in the dust."

Sawyer held Charlie's relationship with Evy in his hand. One word from her long-lost brother and Charlie's chance with Evy would be forever destroyed. And with it—Charlie realized with a sinking feeling in the pit of his stomach—his entire future.

Her brother's eyes hardened. "I thought you liked Evy. That you were her friend. That you might even be falling for her."

"I do. I am." It was true on all counts. "I have."

Sawyer shook the hammer in the air between them. "How could you do this to her? Betray her trust?"

What could Charlie say? He refused to take the easy way out. To explain that once he'd grasped his true feelings for Evy, he'd called off the investigation.

Sawyer beat the hammer into his palm. "She's my sister!"

"I know," Charlie whispered. "You'll never know how much I regret how I handled things."

"You, Charlie Pruitt, are a real piece of work." Sawyer pointed the end of the hammer at him. "Playing her. Letting her believe in you. Taking her trust and trampling on it."

"There's not a name you can call me I haven't already called myself." Charlie braced, broadening his shoulders. "Bring it. I won't fault you."

Sawyer flung the hammer to the ground. "This is going to kill Evy when she finds out." He folded his arms across his chest. "And make no mistake, she will find out what you've done."

He raised his arms shoulder-width and let them drop. "This is Kiptohanock." Sawyer grimaced. "You can't flush a toilet at one end of town and not expect everyone at the other end to hear about it soon."

Exactly what had kept Charlie awake until the wee hours each night since he learned the truth about Evy's identity.

"Why didn't you tell her when she revealed her big secret?"

"Because…" Charlie slumped. "Because I was afraid of losing her." He gulped. "And I can't stand to see her hurt."

"That makes two of us." Sawyer's mouth thinned. "But she's going to hear about it one way or the other. Better that she hears it from you."

Charlie lifted his gaze from the ground. "You're not going to tell her?"

"Not my secret to tell." Sawyer rolled his neck, working out the kinks. "I do appreciate, however, you trying to stop my wife from making everything worse by walking away from it when you did."

"You know about that, too?"

"Honey and I don't make a habit of keeping secrets from each other. Once the floodgate opened on this one, she didn't hold anything back."

Sawyer jutted his jaw. "We'll get past this. We always do." He shook his head. "Life with Honey Duer Kole for sure is never boring." He smiled. "I knew what I was signing up for. No regrets." He shrugged. "What can a guy do when he loves a woman like that?"

What indeed?

Charlie needed to come clean with Evy. Before she heard the truth from someone else. He'd beg for her forgiveness. Grovel. Plead. And pray for a second chance to rebuild her trust in him.

Whatever it took to make sure the best thing that ever happened to him didn't walk away from him for good.

Leaving Sawyer sweating in the noonday sun,

he headed toward the barnyard, determined finally to admit the truth to Evy.

But everything else was forgotten as he spotted Evy—her arm slung around Honey's waist—struggling up the incline from the tidal creek around the corner of the house.

"Charlie!" Evy's face brightened in relief. "We need your help. Honey's gone into labor."

Chapter Fifteen

Clinging to Evy's arm, Honey took a sharp breath as if someone had socked her in the gut.

Evy took an automatic glance at her wristwatch. "The contractions are coming so close together."

Charlie gaped.

"Did you hear me?" Evy growled. "Don't stand there with your mouth hanging open. Help me, Charlie."

As the contraction eased, Honey went limp against Evy's side.

Charlie rushed forward and took hold of Honey's other arm. "What's going on?"

Evy rolled her eyes. "What does it look like is going on? Tea and crumpets with the queen? She's having a baby, Charlie."

Charlie dropped Honey's arm like it was radioactive. "She can't be having a baby. Her due date isn't till…" His gaze darted to Honey, who was breathing in through her nose and exhaling through her pursed lips.

"Till November…" Honey wheezed.

Evy shrugged. "Babies come when they come. Baby Kole is only a few weeks early. So deal, Deputy Pruitt." She scanned the yard. "Have you seen Sawyer?"

Charlie helped Evy steer Honey toward the parked cars. "He's on the fence line in the pasture."

"We need to get him here." Evy bit her lip. "Fast."

"Right."

Propping Honey against the hood of the patrol car, he rounded the engine and poked his head through the driver's side window. He pressed the horn—three short blasts followed by three long bursts plus three short jabs.

Evy smiled at him through the windshield. "Great thinking, Deputy. SOS."

"Figured it'd be right up the alley of an ex-Coastie like Sawyer."

Honey bit back a low moan. "Whatever works."

Sawyer raced across the meadow. "What's wrong? What's happened?"

"It's okay," Evy called as he joined them.

Honey groaned as another contraction gripped her.

Sawyer's eyes went wide. "The baby?" Honey clung to his arm and Evy's for support.

"It's okay, Sawyer." Evy rubbed Honey's shoulder. "Baby Kole has decided to make an early appearance."

"Honey, sweetheart?" Sawyer's voice choked. "It doesn't look okay to me. Something's wrong."

Evy shook her head. "I'm no doctor, but it appears everything is proceeding normally. We need to get her to the hospital ASAP."

"Normally?" Sawyer's voice rose an octave. "It doesn't look like everything is normal. She's in pain."

Evy ignored him. "Do you have your bag packed for the hospital, Honey? Did you leave it at the inn?"

Honey clutched her abdomen. "In...the...truck..."

"Always prepared. Although I'd expect no less from the wife of an ex-Coastie." Evy rubbed small circles on the small of Honey's back. "Ready to welcome Baby Kole to the world?"

Sawyer raked his hand over his head. "This can't be happening."

Charlie had gone pale.

Wimps, the both of them. Good thing God

had given women the privilege and responsibility of bringing new life into His world.

Evy sniffed. "Oh, it's happening, brother dear. Happening right now." She glanced toward Sawyer's truck. "Can you drive?"

"Uh…uh…" Sawyer lifted his shaking hands and stared at them. As if he'd never noticed his appendages before.

Evy blew out an exasperated breath. No help from that quarter. "Fine. Here's the plan, then. We'll stretch Honey out in the backseat of Charlie's cruiser—"

Charlie went rigid. "Hold on there!"

Sawyer straightened. "Wait a minute—"

"I'll ride shotgun in the front seat. You can help Honey in the back." Her eyes darted to Sawyer's stunned features. "On second thought, you ride shotgun. I'll help Honey."

Charlie's jaw jutted. "Why *my* car?"

Her gaze cut to him. "That way you can turn on the siren and step on the gas. We'll get her to the hospital faster."

"But…but—"

Evy tightened her lips. "No buts, Deputy Pruitt."

Charlie sagged against the cruiser. "Suppose she delivers on my upholstery?"

Sawyer winced. "Sorry, man. I hear you."

Honey planted her hands on her hips. "Really, guys?"

Evy peered over the top of her glasses at the men. "Seriously?"

Charlie shuffled. "We have to clean our own patrol vehicles, you know."

Evy tossed her hair, whiplashing Charlie in the face with her ponytail. "Get a grip, the both of you. Help me get Honey inside this car right now, and let's get on the road."

Charlie swallowed hard. Sawyer gulped.

She tapped her wristwatch with her finger. "Time's wasting. Or would you *gentlemen*—and I'm using that term with a great deal of irony—rather deliver the baby yourselves on the side of Highway 13?"

At that, total panic creased both men's faces. They fell into each other in their haste to open the car door.

Evy helped Honey fold into the backseat. She scooted in after Honey.

"Useless." Evy shook her head. "Worse than useless."

She draped the seat belt over Honey's protruding belly and clicked it in place. "Don't want anything to happen to mom and baby en route."

Charlie and Sawyer remained where she'd left them.

"Well, don't just stand there." She gestured. "Get in and drive."

The guys shook themselves, breaking free of their paralysis. Sawyer jumped into the front passenger seat. Charlie threw himself into the driver's side. He cranked the ignition. He raced the motor.

Honey flinched and grabbed for her stomach.

"Breathe, Honey…" Evy laced her fingers in Honey's hand. "Hang on to me and breathe."

"Hee-hee-hee…" Honey panted.

"That's right," Evy encouraged. "Ha-ha-ha…"

Sawyer turned around in the seat and reached for Honey. Charlie's chest heaved as he put the car into Drive. Neither of them looked so good.

"Don't you dare faint on me, Sawyer Kole," Evy hissed. "Some Coastie you are."

"Ex-Coastie," Sawyer whispered between gritted teeth. "Right now I'm a husband." His gaze locked onto Evy's. "A grateful brother and a soon-to-be dad."

Charlie veered toward the road, churning gravel and sending a cloud of dust in their wake.

Evy patted Sawyer's arm slung across the seat. "You're going to be a wonderful dad."

Some of the fear receded from his eyes. "You think so?"

Evy smiled. "I know so."

Charlie gunned the engine as they passed underneath the arch of the crossbars where the farm ended and the road began. Hitting the pavement, the vehicle lurched. Evy felt the bottom of her stomach drop weightless as the car went airborne for a second.

Honey gasped. Sawyer jerked around and gripped the armrest as the car fell to earth with a jolt.

Charlie's mouth twisted. "Sorry…"

"Get us there quick, but get us there alive, dude…" Sawyer shuddered.

"Take a breath, guys." Evy widened her eyes. "Like this—ha-ha-ha…"

Charlie's incredulous gaze found hers in the rearview mirror.

"I'm serious." She hummed a few bars from *Bonanza.* "Time to cowboy up, Deputy Pruitt."

On Seaside Road, Charlie hit the siren. The fallow fields and white farmhouses flew by on either side. On Highway 13, he wove expertly through the Sunday afternoon traffic.

Fortunately, they were going in the opposite direction from the 'come here traffic headed for the bridge after a weekend on the Shore. Charlie grabbed the mic on the console and called in their ETA to the hospital.

The contractions were closer and more wrenching when Charlie barreled into the Emergency Room entrance at the hospital. The nurses and orderlies were waiting as he pulled to a screeching halt under the portico.

Evy scrambled out first, giving the staff access to Honey. They placed her in a wheelchair and headed toward the interior.

Honey snagged Evy's hand. "Thank you, Evy. For everything."

Evy squeezed her hand before letting go.

Sawyer paused at the sliding doors. "Evy?"

Evy touched his shoulder. "Go on. You'll be fine."

A strange look crossed Sawyer's face. "Don't you go anywhere, you hear?"

"I wouldn't miss this for the world, big bro."

Sawyer swung to Charlie. "And thanks, Pruitt. For everything."

Charlie shrugged. "No problem. 'Serve and Protect' is my middle name."

That brought a smile to Sawyer's rugged features. "Take good care of my sister."

"Always, Kole. Goes without saying."

Sawyer disappeared inside.

Charlie scrubbed the back of his neck. "Got to move the cruiser. Ride with me to the parking lot?"

"Sure." Evy climbed into the passenger seat.

Palming the wheel, he headed toward the parking garage. "Just how bad is the state of my upholstery?"

She punched his biceps. Hard.

"Ow…" He massaged his muscle. "Just kidding. A little."

He steered into a vacant spot and parked. "You did great, Evy Shaw." He made a motion at the empty space between them.

With a smile, she slid over and inserted her arm in the crook of his elbow. "All in all, you didn't do so badly yourself, Charles Everett Pruitt."

"Don't forget the Third part."

She made sure he saw her roll her eyes. "SuperDeputy to the rescue."

He laughed. "More like librarian to the rescue. You seem remarkably knowledgeable for someone who's spent a lifetime with her nose in a book."

She play-slapped his biceps again.

He inched back, hands raised off the wheel in surrender. "Okay. Okay. A librarian with her very cute nose stuck in a book." And he tweaked the tip of her nose.

"The library in Miami hosted Red Cross training." She fluttered her lashes. "I couldn't help but train, too."

A wry smile lifted the corners of his eyes. "Red Cross certification. Five languages. The surprises keep coming. What can't you do, Evy Jane Shaw?"

Without stopping to think, she leaned closer. Probably because she didn't stop to think, her lips parted. His eyes darkened. He tilted his head. His breath fanned her cheek.

But then she sat back. "Rain check? I'm about to become an aunt."

He smiled. "Here's hoping it rains very soon."

A nurse directed them to the waiting room. Charlie dialed the numbers, but it was Evy who called Honey's father, Seth Duer. Then her sister Amelia. Followed by her other sister, Caroline.

"Better let the reverend know and the hens, too. Sawyer will appreciate the posthospital meals." Charlie grinned. "I know I did."

Evy hit a number on speed dial. "There's a much more efficient way to spread the word."

Charlie arched his eyebrow. "The Kiptohanock grapevine?"

"You got it." She held the phone to her ear. "Mrs. Davenport?"

Thirty minutes later, the waiting room was standing room only. When the Duer clan arrived, Evy rose from her chair. She knotted her fingers.

For the first time she quavered, dreading the inevitable confrontation. Should she leave? Neither Caroline or Amelia was her biggest fan. Would being here mar the occasion for the family? But she'd promised Sawyer she'd stay.

Charlie stood with her. "You have as much right to be here as any of them," he whispered. "I've got your back, Shaw." And shoulder to shoulder with him, Evy took strength from his strength.

But the Duers—as only the Duers could—surprised Evy. Amelia and Caroline approached, arms outstretched.

Blinking rapidly, Evy was enfolded in their warm Duer embrace. "You—you heard?"

Seth shook Charlie's hand and hooked his arm around Evy. "In my book, any sister of Sawyer's is family." His bristly gray mustache lifted as he grinned.

"I'm sorry I didn't reveal the truth of my real identity before. I wasn't trying to be deceitful. But I didn't want to intrude." She took a ragged breath. "I was afraid."

Caroline clasped Evy in her arms. "Believe me, I understand."

Her big brown eyes—so like Honey's—ping-ponged between the other members of her family. "But all that matters is that you're here, and we're about to become aunts." She squealed in a way highly uncharacteristic of the sophisticated aquatic veterinarian Evy had hitherto known.

Amelia—the tough-as-nails former tomboy—clasped her hands under her chin and bounced in her flats. "Our baby sister is having a baby."

Caroline latched on to Amelia, who latched on to Evy, and together they jumped up and down. Evy was glad she'd worn her Keds today.

Seth chuckled. "You girls."

Charlie smiled. "Women…"

Seth crossed his arms across his flannel shirt. "Can't live with 'em. Don't want to ever live without 'em."

Blushing, Evy pushed her glasses up the bridge of her nose. The Duers plopped into adjacent chairs.

Catching her eye, Charlie winked. Hooking one thumb in his gun belt, he tipped an imaginary hat in the air with his other hand.

"A white hat suits you, Charles Pruitt," she said.

He rolled his tongue in his cheek. "Why, thank ya kindly, little missy."

She laughed at his attempt at a Western drawl. He was a good guy. The best. Her heart thrummed in her chest. Her good guy?

It was with a great deal of applause that Sawyer ventured into the waiting room later to announce the birth of Daisy Marian Kole. Marian, after Honey's deceased mother.

And Daisy, after Sawyer and Evy's mother. Sawyer's eyes locked onto Evy's. Her eyes moistened.

Two by two, the nurses allowed visitors into

Honey's room. When it was Evy's turn, she hung back in the doorframe, allowing Caroline to surge ahead. Propped against the pillows, Honey glowed.

Swaddled in Honey's arms, Evy's niece was all fair skin, rosebud lips and—

Evy's breath hitched at Daisy's patch of white-blond hair standing on its short ends. Sawyer flashed Evy a grin.

Honey smiled at Evy. "Another towhead. Like her Aunt Evy." She motioned Evy forward. "And I for one couldn't be more thrilled."

When Evy held her niece for the first time, something melted in her heart.

Charlie departed soon after with Sawyer to retrieve Sawyer's truck from Keller's farm and officially clock out from his shift. Seth left to tag team with Amelia's husband, Braeden, and Caroline's husband, Weston, on kid duty with Max, Izzie and Patrick—who was no longer the youngest in the ever-expanding Duer clan.

Evy headed down the hall to the vending machine to allow the sisters some private time. Charlie had asked her to wait for him until he changed out of his uniform and returned to the hospital. He'd said he had something he needed to talk over with her.

Perusing the snack options, she hummed the opening bars to *Bonanza*. And for good measure threw in the theme songs for *Star Trek* and *Big Valley*.

She inserted the coins into the slot. And watched the bag of Doritos drop. She wondered what he wanted to discuss. She smiled. Maybe just an excuse for him to claim the rain check she'd given him earlier.

Bending, she reached inside the flap door and extracted the bag of corn chips. Without a cloud in the sky, a rain check sounded like fun. Tingles like ladybugs frolicked across her arms as another thought suddenly occurred to her.

Perhaps he wanted to *tell* Evy something important.

Evy plodded toward the maternity ward again. Her Keds made slapping noises against the tile. She tore open the bag.

Something important like…? Like how she'd opened new worlds for him. The world of literature…

And the world of love. Evy stopped as pleasurable thoughts flitted across her mind.

Outside Honey's room, she detected the sound of raised voices. With an odd sensation of déjà vu, she hesitated. But Charlie's name halted Evy in her tracks.

"Back at the farm, I thought Charlie had already…" Honey sighed. "Oh, no."

Amelia cleared her throat. "We owe it to Charlie to let him be the one to tell Evy the truth."

Evy trembled. What truth?

Caroline's cultured voice rose. "We were crazy to think this could remain a secret. Truth has a way of coming out."

What secret?

"I'm ashamed of being part of this conspiracy." Amelia's voice rasped. "We should've never asked him to spy on the librarian."

Evy crushed the bag in her hand. Blinding pain ripped through her. Charlie had befriended her, joined the book club, made her believe she was important to him, special, so he could...

Just so he could unmask her identity?

Her breath came in rapid pants. How could she have been so gullible? So naive?

A sudden longing washed over her. For the sanctuary of library walls. For her parents. For the soothing, certain comfort of her books. For everything right and true she'd believed in.

Like Charlie?

She had to get out of here. Before they discovered she'd overheard. Evy pushed away from the wall. Her sneakers squeaked against the floor.

"Did you hear that noise?" Honey's voice lifted. "Is someone out there?"

Evy ran for the elevator. She couldn't bear their pity, the truth of her stupidity in their eyes.

Her stupidity in believing someone like Deputy Pruitt could actually be interested in a bookworm librarian like her.

Had she bored him senseless? She jogged past the gurneys cluttering the corridor.

She jabbed the elevator button and squeezed her eyes shut. How he must have clenched his teeth as she'd forced him to read one dreary classic after another.

Or worse, maybe he'd laughed at her wide-eyed wonder. At how easy it was to deceive her. To trick her into revealing parts of herself she'd never admitted to anyone before—not even to herself.

She tapped her foot against the linoleum, waiting for the doors to open. He probably laughed himself silly at her pathetic eagerness, mooning over him like a schoolgirl. She was nothing but an inexperienced simpleton.

When the doors opened, so did her eyes. Opened in more ways than one. Cheeks burning, Evy stepped into the empty elevator.

Not so smart, are you, Evy Shaw? Take a page from Deputy Duplicitous. Guard your heart. Trust no one.

In hindsight, the long look Sawyer had given her outside the emergency room suddenly made sense. Her mouth flattened. Unlike her eyesight, hindsight was always a bitter twenty-twenty.

Her heart thumped against her ribs. She felt like a fool. Her hand shook as she hit the button to close the elevator doors.

As the elevator dropped to ground level, her gut sank, too. When the doors slid open, she staggered out. Why had she ever believed Charlie could be falling in love with her?

His hair still damp from a shower, Charlie sauntered through the emergency room entrance. His face lit at the sight of her. "Hey there, gorgeous."

She balled her fist. Chips and paper crackled. And she threw the open bag, chips ground to smithereens in her fury, into his face.

Charlie staggered backward, raising his arm a fraction of a second too late to ward off the fragmented corn chips. "What in the world, Evy, darlin'?"

Somehow, tiny as she was, she got in his face. She skewered her finger into his chest. "Don't you call me that, you big, stinking, lying con artist." Every word punctuated with a jab.

He hunched his shoulders. So she knew. He took a deep breath.

Someone had beaten him to the punch. In a weird way, he was relieved. Time to own up to the truth. Do damage control.

He opened his palms. "If you'd let me explain—"

"There's no excuse for what you pulled," she hissed.

"You're right. Totally right. But—"

"No buts." She folded her arms across her T-shirt. "You are a cad. And a scoundrel. And a—"

"Right on all counts." The doors whooshed open behind him. "We can't stand here blocking traffic." He took hold of her arm.

She wrenched free. "Don't you touch me, you jerk. What happened to 'Serve and Protect'?" She scowled. "Or does that only apply to the 'been here, born here's?"

"I never meant—"

"What did you mean, then? I trusted you. I believed in you."

His heart ached at the total disillusionment on her face. The pain he'd caused. "I was doing a favor for a friend. But I—"

"You lied."

"Not everything was a lie." He swallowed. "All my feelings were true. Everything we shared."

Her nostrils flared. "Do you know the meaning of truth, Pruitt? How long were you going to let me play the fool?" Evy's lip curled. "How long did you intend to keep the charade of our relationship going? How long before you dropped out of the book club? And stopped coming by the library?"

"I should've told you. I knew I could trust you even before you told me why you were here."

"Then why didn't you?" She narrowed her eyes. "I'll tell you why. Because you'd been played before. And in your heart of hearts, you still weren't willing to trust me."

"I'll do anything for us to get past this, Evy."

She sneered. "I'd be an idiot to stand here while you tell me more lies to make yourself feel better." Hurt shimmered in her eyes. "Why, Charlie? Why didn't you tell me the truth? I believed you were…" Evy shook herself. "It doesn't matter what I thought. 'Cause I was wrong. Where it counts, you're not one of the good guys after all. I hope you and your badge will be happy together."

Then she walked away.

His heart lurched. "Wait. Evy, don't go. How will you get back to—"

She removed her cell phone from her pocket and didn't bother turning around. "I'm sure one of my real friends will give me a ride."

He fell against the stucco wall. He'd lost her. His worst fears were realized. And he understood that his real issue hadn't been a lack of trust in Evy. But ultimately, a lack of faith in God.

Charlie deserved to be alone. Forever.

Chapter Sixteen

Early the next morning, it didn't take Evy long to compose a short email of resignation to Mrs. Davenport. Or to pack her few possessions in the room she rented at the Crockett farm. Barely holding it together, she said goodbye to a tearful Miss Pauline, who begged Evy to reconsider.

Evy unlocked the stout library door as Kiptohanock awakened from its long, sleepy night. A long, sleepless night for her.

She paused on the porch to take in the view one last time as the sun bathed the tiny fishing hamlet in light. Streaks of lavender and rose pink banded the horizon. In the distance, the barrier islands gleamed like a string of pearls.

Recreational and fishing boats bobbed in the harbor. The post office. The outfitter and boat repair shop. The Coast Guard station flags fluttered in the crisp, autumn sea breeze.

Home. The closest she'd ever come to finding a place to belong. Where she'd made friends, found long-lost family members and discovered a purpose beyond herself.

She glanced beyond the gazebo on the village green to the gingerbread-trimmed homes. Overarching the side lanes, the tree canopy was a kaleidoscope of color. And beneath the fiery reds and golden yellows of an Eastern Shore autumn lay Charlie's house.

Evy bit her lip and pushed open the library door. She'd never get to see the lovely Victorian home glow against the stark, bare beauty of winter.

She stumbled into the foyer. Nor read to the children at Story Hour. There were many things she'd never do again. At least not here in Kiptohanock. Never again with Charlie.

A small sob escaped from between her clenched lips. She put her hand over her mouth. It was the death of dreams. The death of everything she'd only just begun to imagine could be hers.

She balled her hand against her thigh. She must have been delusional to believe a man like Deputy Pruitt and someone like her could ever… An image of the window seat in Charlie's house pummeled her like a fist.

The coulda's, shoulda's, woulda's ate her alive. Her life in Kiptohanock was over.

She'd chosen sensibility—emotion—over good sense. And look where that had gotten her. Heartbroken. But she still had her pride. She couldn't stay here. Not one minute longer than she had to.

Evy walked among the library shelves one last time. She collected a few personal items. Set things to rights for the town's new librarian, whoever he or she might be. Took one final look around.

Her beloved books would no longer be enough. In Kiptohanock, she'd savored what it was like to be enveloped in the warm embrace of friends.

The library could no longer be her safe place in a crazy, uncaring world. Charlie had spoiled that for her. Providing a tantalizing glimpse of something more.

Her stomach knotted. She'd spoiled Kiptohanock for herself. By trusting. By believing in Charlie.

But never again would she play invisible for anyone. That's why she had to leave. In a town the size of Kiptohanock, she and Charlie would cross paths repeatedly. And that wasn't something she'd willingly subject herself to on a weekly basis.

Evy was done with being overlooked. With being forgettable.

She'd banish herself from Kiptohanock. For the sake of self-preservation, banish herself from Charlie Pruitt. And from the silly, ridiculous love that had been doomed from the beginning. Unlike the Duer sisters times three, there'd be no fairy-tale ending for her.

"Evy?"

She glanced up as the door creaked open. Her salt-and-pepper chignon askew, Mrs. Davenport rushed inside still wearing her bedroom slippers. Evy blinked at the usually immaculate Mrs. Davenport's disheveled appearance.

Mrs. Davenport's face sagged in relief. "I was so afraid you'd already left."

Evy's heart hitched. Mrs. Davenport had been a good friend, too. Her first real friend in Kiptohanock, welcoming a 'come here from nowhere.

"I'm sorry to leave the library patrons in a lurch." Evy swallowed against the sudden lump in her throat. "I—I can't stay here. I appreciate the committee's confidence in me. Offering me this most wonderful of opportunities, but…but…"

She blinked away the treacherous tears. She'd thought—hoped—she'd shed the last of them in the wee hours of the morning. "I'm so sorry.

Perhaps one of the other candidates you interviewed—" She gulped.

Mrs. Davenport came around the desk. "We didn't bother to interview anyone else after you." She wrapped her arm around Evy's shoulders. "Don't worry about the library. I'll staff it in your absence. Until you clear your head and come back to us."

"I'm not coming back."

Mrs. Davenport sighed. "I heard what happened between you and Charlie."

Of course she had. This was Kiptohanock, and Mrs. Davenport was its grapevine.

"Did you know about him pretending to be my—my..." Evy stiffened. "How stupid can I get, to think a man like him would join a Jane Austen book club? Did everyone know but me?"

Mrs. Davenport squeezed Evy's hand. "No, honey. And I don't think Charlie Pruitt was pretending."

Evy pulled away.

"I see the way he looks at you." Mrs. Davenport wagged her finger. "I've known the deputy since he played tiny-tyke football. That boy is completely smitten with you."

Evy slung her tote bag over her shoulder. "SuperDeputy played me. In a weird sort of way, I get why Honey started this, but what I can't understand is, after Charlie got to know me, how

he could continue to investigate me while—"
Her cheeks burned.

"All the while romancing the truth out of you?"

Evy scowled.

"But where will you go, Evy?"

"I don't know exactly. San Francisco?"
She shrugged. "Maybe I'll join my parents in France."

She hugged Mrs. Davenport. "This has been the best…the most…"

Mrs. Davenport cupped Evy's face between her hands. "I wish you'd stay, but I understand why you feel the need to go. Just remember, with or without Charles Everett Pruitt the Third, there are people here who love you and who will miss you. Including yours truly."

Tears threatened to spill onto Evy's cheeks. She had to get out of here—before she lost the will to leave. "I—I won't forget, Mrs. Davenport. I love you, too. But I have to go."

With an arm around Evy's shoulder, Mrs. Davenport walked her to the door.

On the threshold, Evy hesitated. "You'll finish the book club for me? I saved my favorite for last. We haven't discussed *Emma* yet."

"Consider it done."

With a final promise to send her contact information once she got settled, Evy slipped out onto the porch and closed the door behind her.

It was time to boldly go…somewhere else. To cast off the uncertainty of her right to exist. To be Jane. To be Evy. Perhaps, at long last, to find a place where she could be both.

And discover her own happily-ever-after. One thing she'd never leave behind, though? Her eyes skimmed the steeple brushing the sky above Kiptohanock.

The peace. The joy. The hope she'd take with her wherever she went from now on. Despite everything that had happened—past and present— God was still so very good.

There was one other consideration… Sawyer had spent the night at the hospital with Honey. Evy thought about stopping by the hospital on her way out of town, but rejected the idea immediately.

Riverside Hospital was in the opposite direction from the Bay Bridge Tunnel and the mainland. But more importantly, she hated goodbyes. She felt nauseated contemplating telling Sawyer goodbye. Her reaction, probably a carryover from being wrenched apart as children. When she believed she'd said goodbye to him and to Jane Kole forever.

No more guilt. No more pretending. She sent him a text.

Can't stay here. I'll call when I get to wherever. Not goodbye forever. Goodbye, sweet brother, just for now.

She stared at the words. It was better this way. She'd call Dixie on the other side of the bridge. When she was out of reach of anyone trying to persuade her to stay. She pushed her glasses higher onto the bridge of her nose.

And hit Send.

She was so sick of goodbyes. Her life had been one goodbye after another. It was past time to find somewhere she could call home. A place filled with hello.

After Evy walked away outside the hospital, Charlie went straight to headquarters and volunteered to do another shift. He didn't want to go home. He didn't know how he was ever going to face the yawning emptiness of his house and his heart.

So he spent a long night on duty. A long night when nothing much happened in Accomack County. Great news for the citizens. Bad news for Charlie. Who had nothing to do but examine in minute detail how he'd blown things with Evy.

Charlie replayed every conversation they'd ever had in his head. Berated himself for every missed opportunity. But he'd been so afraid that if he told Evy the truth, he'd lose her.

He hunkered inside the patrol vehicle. He'd lost her anyway. And he had no one to blame but himself.

Charlie's head fell back onto the headrest as he peered into the early dawn. He'd rationalized he was protecting Evy from hurt. But the only one he'd really been protecting was himself.

She'd never trust him again. Not that he blamed her. He winced, recalling the hurt and disbelief in her eyes when she learned the truth of why he'd pretended to be her friend. He ached inside.

Charlie had enjoyed being her friend. He scrubbed his hand over his beard shadow. Who knew a *Bonanza* kind of guy would fall in love with a Jane Austen kind of girl? He swallowed.

He'd fallen in love with Evy Jane. The quirky librarian. The delightful girly-girl. The ponytail. The glasses. The way her eyes lit up—his heart thudded—when she looked at him across a crowded book club meeting.

Charlie groaned. She'd never look at him that way again. And it sucked the life out of him thinking of everything his insufferable pride had cost him. Cost the both of them.

For he'd lost something irretrievably precious when she stalked away from him outside the hospital. He could no longer deny the depth and scope of his feelings for Evy. He loved her. He wanted her in his life so badly, he'd do anything to earn her forgiveness.

Maybe after she simmered down, she'd listen to his explanation of how things had gotten out of control. How he never meant to hurt her. How events snowballed and before he realized it, he'd fallen head over heels in love with her.

His conscience smote him. The words from Scripture hammered his brain. About what love was. And what love was not.

Love rejoiced with truth. Love bore all things. Believed all things. Endured all things. Love didn't fail. He had failed Evy in the most fundamental of ways. And without her love, Charles Everett Pruitt the Third was nothing.

Yet love also didn't give up.

Charlie remembered the familiar mantra of his football days. *Don't give in. Never quit. Keep moving forward.*

He clamped his lips together. Charles Everett Pruitt the Third was nothing if not persuasive. He'd wear her down. He'd beg for mercy. Dog her at church and in the village.

When it came to winning back Evy's respect, he'd do whatever it took. He'd become a frequent, card-carrying library customer. Maybe she'd have pity on him. Give him another chance to be her friend.

And after a while, maybe she'd forgive him. Trust him. Love him the way he loved her.

God, I messed up so badly. Forgive me. I don't deserve a wonderful person like Evy. But I love her...

He slumped in his seat. "I love her so much. Soften her heart. Help her to let me into her life one more time. Show me what I can do to regain her faith in me."

It was Evy who'd helped him let go of his bitterness. With her fresh eyes of new faith, she showed Charlie the way back to the God of second chances. Sweet Evy... *God, would you allow me a second chance with her?*

He was driving north to the station to clock out when his cell rang. He snatched it off the console. A text from Honey.

Do something. She's getting away.

Charlie frowned. What was Honey talking about? Who was getting away?

His phone buzzed with another incoming text. Charlie's eyes widened. Since when did Sawyer Kole text him?

Call me. Now.

Sawyer probably wanted his turn at reaming Charlie out for hurting his beloved sister. Which he more than deserved.

He pulled into a gas station to place the call. Teeth gritted, he redialed. Step one in his long-overdue twelve-step program of humility.

The Coastie cowboy picked up on the first ring.

Charlie took a breath. "Sawy—"

"Do you love my sister, Pruitt?"

"What?"

"Answer the question," Sawyer growled. "Do you love her or not? After the stunt you and my beloved but delusional wife pulled, I'm not so sure."

Charlie gripped the phone in his hand. "I love Evy a lot."

"What does *a lot* mean to you, Pruitt? What're your intentions toward my baby sister?"

"I—I…" Charlie's heart hammered. "I'd gladly spend the rest of my life making it up to her if she'd marry me. Be my wife. Bear my—"

"Spare me the details," Sawyer grunted. "I get the picture. Now it's my turn to clue you in—if you don't do something quick, she'll be anybody's wife but yours."

Charlie tensed. "What are you talking about? Has something happened to Evy?"

"She resigned her job, packed her stuff and is headed off-Shore."

Charlie's heart raced. "But—"

"Got a text from her. I called her back. She told me in no uncertain terms she was driving to the mainland, then California or Paris—she wasn't exactly forthcoming with the info. And she hung up. She won't answer the rest of my calls. I'd go after her, but Honey and the baby are being released—"

"Where was she when you talked to her?" Fear and panic exploded in Charlie's skull.

"Driving out of Kiptohanock. She's probably on 13 by now and headed south to the bridge. I'm not sure what you can do, but if anyone can convince her to stay, it'll be you." Sawyer heaved a sigh. "Beats me, but—for some reason I'm totally unable to fathom—my otherwise brilliant sister seems to be in love with you. No accounting for taste, I guess, huh?"

Whereas before Charlie would've bristled, he now knew Sawyer Kole well enough to catch the wry amusement in his voice.

"You wouldn't mind then, if Evy and me—"

"Deputy Pruitt, if you return my only sister to the Kiptohanock fold, I'll gladly dance at your wedding." Sawyer sniffed. "After I teach you how to do a proper two-step, of course. Can't have you disgracing the Kole family name."

And in his words, Sawyer not only offered him an olive branch but also bestowed his cowboy blessing.

Evy and Honey had been right about the ex-Coastie. He was a good guy. A great guy. A man worth knowing. No matter how things worked out with Evy, Charlie would consider it an honor to be Sawyer's friend.

Sawyer blew out a breath. "I'm not sure what you can do to stop her—"

"You leave it to me." Charlie's mouth flattened. "I've got this."

Sawyer laughed. "Somehow I had a feeling you would. Go do your thing, Deputy. Bring back Cotton."

"Roger that." Charlie clicked off and palmed the wheel. Tires screeching, he wheeled out of the gas station and headed south on 13.

He reached for the mic and put in a call to the station. Charlie wasn't about to allow the best person outside of God who ever happened to him to get away. Not on his watch.

Dispatch put Charlie through to his boss. Charlie got right to the point of what he needed.

"I realize this request is highly unusual, sir. Unorthodox. And if it means resigning my position and losing my career, I understand."

"She means that much to you, does she, Pruitt?"

"Yessir. She does."

The sheriff laughed. "Been there, son. While I can't allocate taxpayer dollars in the pursuit of love, I can authorize law enforcement to be on the lookout for someone Deputy Pruitt needs to question." His boss chuckled, his voice gravelly. "I'm assuming that once apprehended, you do have questions for the suspect. Or at least, one all-important question, Deputy?"

Charlie gripped the wheel as the intersection at the town of Painter blurred past his window. "I do indeed, sir. And I'd be much obliged for any help you could spare."

"Got her number, by chance?"

Charlie smiled. "Emblazoned on my brain." He rattled off Evy's license plate number. "Thank you, sir."

"No problem. Bring back the girl, Deputy."

As Charlie sped past Nassawadox, the un-official BOLO went out over the radio to his brothers in blue on the two-county peninsula to locate the pretty blonde librarian. Minutes later, his hope was rewarded when good friend Thad Walters responded.

"Vehicle spotted. Outside the Cackle and Crow in Cheriton. Stop and detain? Please advise. Standing by."

Charlie's heart thumped. Last exit before the bridge. She must've stopped for breakfast before heading over the seventeen-mile bridge and tunnel expanse. He had a bad feeling that if they didn't catch her this side of the mainland, he'd never see her again.

He picked up the mic. "Be advised." He released the button. Charlie set his jaw. He pressed down the button again. "Do not attempt to apprehend. I repeat, do not apprehend. Delay, yes, Trooper Walters."

Thad laughed. "Advise. Is suspect dangerous?"

He flushed. So much for pride. Everyone with a scanner in a two-county radius was no doubt following this development play-by-play.

Charles Everett Pruitt the Third would once again be the laughingstock of the Delmarva Peninsula. But he'd do so and more for a do-over with Evy.

"Be advised suspect is dangerous." He took a breath. "But only to my heart. Suspect must be approached with caution."

"Roger that. Will delay till you arrive and then she's all yours, Deputy Pruitt."

Charlie blew past Exmore.

Oh, how he hoped so.

Chapter Seventeen

After a sleepless night, fatigue caught up with Evy. Facing a long drive over the choppy waters of the Chesapeake Bay, she figured she'd better stop for caffeine while she had the chance.

Plus—despite the fiasco with Charlie—she wasn't eager to put the Shore behind her quite yet. Which made her what?

"A glutton for punishment."

"Excuse me, cupcake?" The waitress's blue-green eyes reminded Evy of the Kiptohanock harbor. "What did you say?"

Evy shook her head. Time to put the past where it belonged, in the past. Including what had been the most wonderful few months of her life.

"Which just shows you how stupid I am."

The waitress paused in the act of pouring

coffee into Evy's to-go cup. "Man trouble, sweetie?"

"Idiot trouble. And I'm not talking only about him."

The waitress nodded with the hard-won wisdom of experience.

Maybe all waitresses by occupational necessity were also psychotherapists. Perhaps Evy should've talked to Dixie before hightailing it out of town.

As Evy paid for the coffee, bells jingled at the front door of the Cackle and Crow. Her gaze flitted to the mirror behind the counter to the tall uniformed figure filling the doorway.

Her heart seized until the deputy removed his trooper hat. Not Charlie. But she recognized the officer. Thad something. They'd met at Riverside Hospital. A friend of Charlie's.

Thad's eyes flicked to the waitress and back to Evy. "Ma'am. Good to see you again."

She nodded. "Officer."

"Your usual cuppa joe and a muffin, Thad?" The waitress lifted the glass lid of the cake stand.

The state trooper's lips curved up, but it was Evy who remained locked in his crosshairs. "You know what I like, Violet."

Evy took a step to leave.

Hands resting on his gun belt, Thad sidestepped and blocked her exit. "Fancy seeing you in Northampton County this morning, Miss Shaw."

"Yes, well…" She stepped left.

So did Thad. She frowned.

He gave her a supercilious smile. "Going somewhere so soon?"

She supposed some girls went for the broad-shouldered man in uniform. But she wasn't most girls. Only man, uniform or in jeans, she went for was Charlie Pruitt.

And that had turned out so well for her. The sooner she got off this peninsula the better.

"If you'll excuse me…"

Legs widening to hip stance, Thad once again effectively cut off her escape. "What's your hurry? I'd love some company on my break."

"I don't think so." She fluttered her hand. "Places to go. People to see."

"That's a shame. Taking a trip over the bridge?"

"Yes, I am."

"A word to the wise, Miss Shaw." He took the white paper bag from the waitress. "Thanks, Violet."

"What word would that be, Officer?"

He fished a five-dollar bill out of his pocket and slid it over the countertop toward Violet. "Rush hour."

Backed against the stool, Evy glared. "That's not a word. That's a phrase. What're you talking about?"

"I stand corrected." He smirked. "I forgot you were that book gal from the Kiptohanock library. But rush hour is something you don't want to get caught in. Not stuck on the bridge with Shore folks headed to jobs in Virginia Beach, or sidelined by Tidewater residents commuting to Norfolk, either. Trust me. Gridlock on the interstate isn't pretty."

Balancing her coffee, she crossed her arms. "I'll take that under advisement, Officer. But I must be on my way."

"How much gas have you got in that Mini Cooper of yours?"

"About a quarter of—" She narrowed her eyes. "How do you know what I drive?"

"Mini Coopers kind of stand out on the Shore. Hospital parking lot, remember?"

Something wasn't right. Until Charlie, men hadn't taken an interest in Evy Shaw. Thad wasn't exactly making a play for her, but something was off.

"No gas station between the bridge and Virginia Beach. If you get trapped in one of those traffic jams, you could be stuck on the highway for an hour or more."

"I appreciate the warning, Officer."

"Thad."

"What? Oh, Thad. But why the sudden—"

"Part of the job, ma'am. I'm here to serve and protect."

She curled her lip. "So I've been told. Thanks for the tip. I'll stop for gas before I go through the toll plaza."

Evy faked to the left. Then dodged right. And managed to scoot past his hulking frame.

She dashed for the door and flung it open with wild abandon. The bells jangled behind her as she fled toward her car. She felt a whoosh of air.

Officer Thad inserted himself between Evy and her vehicle. She stopped midstep and tottered in her heels. He smiled.

Her breath came in short spurts. "What are— Why—?"

"Can't be too careful. I thought I'd check your tire pressure before you head out on your long trip."

She suppressed the desire to groan.

Thad kept up a running monologue about the joys of the Delmarva Peninsula. The fishing. The beaches. The down-home friendliness of the locals.

After checking the tires, he insisted she get behind the wheel so he could check turn signals and rear lights. One step closer toward her goal of driving off-Shore forever, she complied and cranked the engine.

The safety check dragged on as Thad waxed eloquent about the supposed superiority of the Cape Charles, Northampton County library versus, say, the Kiptohanock, Accomack County library.

Which riled her. She wasted another twenty minutes defending Kiptohanock and the entire county of Accomack.

By this point, Thad leaned against her idling car, his snack bag resting on the hood.

She squirmed in her seat. "If that's all, Officer? Thanks so much for your helpfulness, but now I really must be—"

"My niece is having trouble finding books to enjoy. As a book specialist, Miss Shaw, could you make any recommendations?"

She gawked at him through the half-open window. "Books?"

"That's what you do, isn't it?"

"Yes." She gritted her teeth. "That's what I do."

What was the trooper's deal?

"Okay…" She let her breath trickle out slowly from between her lips. "How old is your niece?"

Thad fidgeted. "Eighteen months."

Her mouth fell open. "Eighteen months? She

can't read yet unless…" She reached for the gearshift. "Unless she's a child prodigy."

"She is real smart." Thad chuckled. "Takes after her uncle."

These Shore people were insane. And annoying.

"Goodbye, Officer." She raised the window and shifted into Reverse. "I'll be leaving now."

Just in time, Thad grabbed the paper bag before it slid to the ground.

With a backhanded wave, she eased out of the parking space. What was up with that guy? In the rearview mirror, she spotted Thad speaking into his shoulder mic.

Clicking her seat belt in place—before the trooper stopped her on a safety violation—she pulled onto 13. Time to put the Delmarva Peninsula and perfidious law enforcement officials like SuperDeputy behind her. She dutifully stopped for gas per Thad's timely warning and then headed toward the bridge.

Minutes from the toll plaza, she detected the whine of a police siren. Her eyes flashed to the mirror. The swirling blue light of a police cruiser advanced. Her foot automatically lightened on the accelerator. Her gaze cut left and right. Was the siren meant for her?

What had she done? Her speed was within the posted limits. Maybe the officer was after someone else. But the patrol car kept pace, hugging her bumper. Ignoring the other, slowing vehicles.

If this was Thad again... She rapped the wheel.

Surrendering to the inevitable, she veered off the highway and came to a standstill on a parallel secondary road. The cruiser nosed in behind her Mini Cooper.

Great. Just great. She'd have a ticket to remember her heartbreak here as well. Her shoulders slumped. The cruiser's door opened and closed. Footsteps crunched over gravel.

She fumbled through her purse for her driver's license. A shadow fell across the window. Blocking the bright morning sunshine.

Hitting a button, she rolled the window halfway down. She took one glance. Fury consumed her.

"And here I had hoped never to lay eyes on you again, Charlie Pruitt."

Not the response Charlie had been hoping for. Thad had delayed Evy for as long as he could. Charlie only did catch her vehicle this side of the bridge.

He squared his shoulders. "I wanted to say again that I realize I made a mistake in not telling you the truth from the beginning."

Evy's hands white-knuckled the wheel.

"I was wrong to deceive you. Especially when my gut was telling me to trust you."

She stared straight ahead out the windshield. Her lips flat, she refused to look at him.

"Evy..." His stomach churned. "Please know how sorry I am. I never wanted to hurt you."

She strangled the wheel. Probably what she'd like to do to him if she could get her hands around his throat. "Save it for someone who cares, Deputy." She reached for the gearshift.

Emptiness consumed him. She wasn't ready to listen. He had to do something fast or lose her forever. He wasn't ready to give up on her, or them, yet. Not by a long shot.

"Turn off the ignition, and keep your hands where I can see them."

Her eyes jerked to his. "What?"

"Don't make me repeat myself, Miss Shaw."

He steeled himself against the rapid blinking in those azure-blue eyes of hers. He gave her the hard, intimidating look he'd honed in the academy. A look he saved for offenders. It didn't seem to faze Evy.

Quivering with outrage, she removed her hand from the gearshift. With a flick of her wrist, she turned off the engine.

"There," she grunted. "Satisfied now, Deputy?"

Mouth thinning, he removed the pad from his jacket.

Evy's eyes enlarged. "You're writing me a ticket? But—"

He withdrew a pen from his pocket. "No buts."

"But I haven't done anything," she growled.

He started writing.

Evy's gaze darted to the reflection of his vehicle in the mirror. "You have no jurisdiction, Deputy. I'm in Northampton County."

He kept writing.

"You have no right to detain me."

He didn't bother to answer. Only the scratching of his pen on the paper broke the silence.

"What are you charging me with?" She throttled the wheel. "I wasn't speeding."

He bent over the pad, concentrating on getting the wording right.

"I know for a fact, all you care about is the law."

He lifted his head at the sneer in her voice.

"And my lights and turn signals are in perfect working order."

"I'm afraid I'm going to have to ask you to exit your vehicle now, Miss Shaw."

Her mouth dropped. "You— I... How dare you, Charles Pruitt?"

"Ma'am..."

Her face went fuchsia, almost apoplectic.

Charlie clicked the end of the ballpoint and reinserted it into his uniform pocket. He reached for the door handle at the same moment she shoved it open. He hopscotched backward to avoid being knocked down.

Lunging out of the driver's side, she slammed the car door behind her for good measure. The Mini Cooper rocked. With a flourish, he tore the ticket from the pad and handed it to her.

Teetering in her trademark heels, she snatched the paper from him. He bit back a sigh. She had the loveliest ankles of any woman he'd ever known.

"Read it for yourself." He folded his arms over his chest. "Since I know how much you love to read."

If looks were lethal, he figured he might be lying on the pavement right now—officer down. She glanced at the paper in her hand. She frowned.

He inserted a finger between his neck and the collar of his uniform and tugged. He gulped. She crushed the ticket in her fist and shook it in his face.

The resemblance between the mulish ex-Coastie and Evy was extraordinary. He didn't know why he hadn't seen it immediately. The blue laser glare she threw his way could have reduced a lesser man to cinders.

But Evy Shaw hadn't met stubborn until she'd dealt with Charlie Pruitt.

He placed his hands on either side of his gun belt. "Read it out loud, if you please, Miss Shaw. Don't make me go all Five-0 on you."

Evy's hair blew across her cheek in the breeze blowing off the water. Her eyes shifted to Fisherman's Island beyond the toll plaza. So close and yet so far. Fuming, she brushed the strand of hair out of her face.

Charlie's eyes flickered at the movement of her hand.

And for the first time since being pulled over, something besides anger stirred her heart.

His uniform looked crumpled. His hazel eyes appeared tired. Red-rimmed. As if he'd spent an anguished night since she walked away from him at the hospital.

Which was just too bad. She hadn't exactly had a fun night herself. But she smoothed out the ticket against the fabric of her skirt. A muscle ticked in his lantern jaw.

She held the paper to the light of the sun. And read—per his instructions—aloud. "'I love you.'" She looked at him.

His Adam's apple bobbed in his throat. "Please read the rest, Evy."

Lips pursed, her eyes dropped to the paper. "'Throwing myself on the forgiveness of the court—'"

His arms fell to his sides. He leaned forward. His posture rigid.

Evy's pulse hammered. She refocused on the ticket. "'I'm sentencing myself to the protective custody of my favorite librarian—'"

Her lips twitched. "Get real, Charlie. I'm the only librarian you know."

"The only librarian I want to know." Jaw tight, he pointed his chin at the paper in her hand. "There's more."

She cleared her throat. "'...sentencing myself to the protective custody of my favorite librarian, if she'll have me.'"

Evy studied his set face. The hazel in his eyes had darkened to green. His brow puckered. Their eyes locked. Her stomach did somersaults at the look in his eyes.

She recalled Mrs. Davenport's words about the way Charlie Pruitt looked at her. The look he aimed at her now. A look that set her heart aflutter. A look that curled her toes. A look that almost made Evy believe.

Her gaze fell to the paper. His handwriting

blurred. Treacherous tears threatened to have their way with her. She swayed.

Charlie reached out his hand and then dropped it to his side. "Evy…"

As if he were afraid to touch her. She sniffed. He ought to be afraid.

Yet his voice vibrated with the same longing she felt for him. The hope. The vulnerability. The fear.

She swallowed hard and read the signature line. "'Captured by Love, Deputy Charles Everett Pruitt the Third.'"

A meadowlark trilled from an adjacent field. A lone white farmhouse lay in the distance. And beyond the tree-filled horizon, a tidal creek gleamed like diamonds in the early morning sun. Beckoning. Waiting.

Nowhere on the Shore was ever very far from the water. Her gaze returned to Charlie.

He'd taken off his hat. "I focused on the wrong things first. But I see you, Evy Jane. I see you for who you are."

"Evy or Jane? Who am I, Charlie?" She tilted her head. "Who do you see when you look at me?"

"I see you as both."

Tears sprang to her eyes. She wrapped her arms around herself. The engine made cooling noises.

He moved closer, blocking the wind. "I see a woman made stronger by a tough childhood. A woman refined by the loss of her brother. Her character is as beautiful as her face."

She bit back a sob.

Once again, he reached for her and hesitated, his hand hanging midair between them. Her heart accelerated. She wanted him to touch her, to love her.

He must've seen something in her face because, biting his lip, he touched her face anyway.

She closed her eyes and pressed her cheek into the palm of his hand.

"You are the smartest woman I know. Too smart for the likes of someone like me." His voice went husky. "You've made me into a Jane man for life. An Evy Jane man.

"And I think—" his voice trembled "—I think you've always seen me, too. Really seen me for who I am without the badge." Charlie shrugged his broad shoulders. "I wasn't sure there was a me without the badge until I met you."

His dark hair glistened in the sunlight. "You saw past the Charlie Pruitt I wanted the rest of the world to believe was the real me."

Charlie's eyes dropped. "You saw the me who loves *Bonanza*. Who loves small-town Eastern Shore life. You saw past the hurt and bitterness."

He laid his hat on the roof of the car. "Saw

straight to my heart, where I yearned to find something and someone to believe in again. Made possible because first, you believed in me when I'd lost faith in myself."

She picked up his hat and turned it around in her hands. "I get how you want to serve and protect. SuperDeputy. I admire how you're always there for the people fortunate enough to be called your friends."

His eyes watered. "If I'm SuperDeputy, it's only because of the super God within me. When you walked away last night, I finally understood this great love I feel inside for you. And today, when Sawyer called to tell me you'd gone? I lost all pride as I realized how desolate I'd be if you disappeared from my life forever."

Charlie propped his hands on either side of her body against the car. "Please don't go, Evy. Don't leave your brother and the many people who call you friend." He took a ragged breath. "Please don't leave me—even though I totally screwed up everything between us. Give me another chance to prove how much I really, really love you."

"It's always about proof with you."

"Could you ever forgive me? Believe in me again?"

She trembled, holding the hat between them.

"Even if you don't love me, can you find it in your heart to let me love you, Evy?" He took the hat from her and threw it on the ground. "And I pray maybe one day, you'll learn to love me, too."

She lifted her chin. "I don't see that happening, Charlie."

His face constricting, he let go of her. "E-Evy..." he stammered. "I—"

"You don't have to prove anything to me. And I don't see myself learning to love you one day. It's too late for that."

He inhaled sharply and stepped back.

She grabbed his hand. "Because I already love you." A tear too long suspended fell from her eye and tracked onto her cheek.

He caught the teardrop, and it quivered on the tip of his finger. "You love me?" He said it like he'd never believed anyone ever would.

"Oh, Charlie." She clasped his face between her hands. "I love you. I've always loved you, and I always will." His beard stubble sandpapered her palms.

He crushed her against him. "Oh, Evy," he whispered. "My dearest, truest love."

She glanced skyward at the clear, cloudless blue sky. "Would you look at that?" Smiling, she opened her hands, palms up. "Is that rain?"

Evy stretched forward on her tiptoes. "Maybe time for that rain check?"

Charlie lowered his head. "Definitely, Miss Shaw." His gaze gentled.

Her lips parted. His kiss was tentative, like he expected her to pull away.

But she draped her hands around the back of his neck, drawing his mouth firmly onto hers. And nothing else mattered to Evy in that moment. Nothing but her love for Charlie and his love for her.

Taking a breath, she patted his shoulder. "I used to think I fell hopelessly, totally in love with you somewhere over a plate of egg rolls."

"Egg rolls?" He played with a tendril of her hair. "And here I believed it was because of my Eastern Shore charm, country-boy good looks and SuperDeputy uniform." He gave her a winsome, lopsided smile.

She cocked her head. "Think again."

He quirked his eyebrow. "Not a badge bunny, Miss Shaw?"

She peeked at him over the top of her glasses.

"How about because of my witty repartee?" He grinned. "Or my incisive analysis of the classics?" He frowned. "And what do you mean about *used to*?"

She rolled her eyes at him but snuggled into his towering frame. She brushed an imaginary speck of dust off the lapel of his uniform. "You, Charlie Pruitt, had me at the ring tone for *Bonanza*."

Epilogue

Charlie knew himself to be the most fortunate man alive.

As he glanced around the Pruitt family Thanksgiving table, his gaze alighted upon Evy's upturned face. Her eyes sparkled behind her glasses as his dad became chatty about Zane Grey novels to Bradford Shaw—who, of all people, was also a die-hard Western fiction fan.

Evy winked at Charlie. He watched his mother interact with the coolly elegant Ursula Shaw.

That morning in October, he'd given Evy an official escort back to Kiptohanock from the bridge.

He'd turned on the siren. All the way home. Like a triumphal procession. Because he didn't care who knew—the most wonderful woman on the planet had decided to become his.

That same day, Evy phoned her parents and

told them what she'd done. How she felt. Where she intended to live the rest of her life. And she invited them to be a part of that life if they wanted.

Bradford and Ursula Shaw got on the next plane for Baltimore. They drove from Maryland to Kiptohanock. And there they remained, choosing to spend the rest of their sabbatical getting reacquainted with their daughter.

It had been an awkward reunion at first. Especially when she introduced her brother to them. The aloof Dr. Ursula actually broke down. Which sent Evy into tears. Bradford Shaw apologized for not being willing to take brother and sister both so long ago.

Sawyer had been gracious. Charlie wasn't so sure he could've forgiven as easily the long years of separation and resulting anguish. But when he beheld Sawyer holding Daisy in his arms, Charlie understood that to do anything less would only spoil Sawyer's ability to enjoy the gifts God had given him now.

Charlie realized that in their own way—the surprisingly inarticulate way of people who were supposed to be masters of the English language—her parents indeed loved Evy. Even if they sometimes failed to communicate how much.

The last month had been healing for Evy. She

blossomed into the woman Charlie suspected God always intended her to be. She'd stopped doing that melding, invisible Romulan cloaking-device thing.

Yes…thanks to Evy, he'd acquired an appreciation for all things Trekkie.

He'd grown a lot also. In his faith. And in his great love for a particular librarian.

The book club successfully finished its fall session. *Emma* turned out to be his personal favorite, too. The women expressed a desire to continue with another series after the holidays. And he wasn't above admitting to a certain fondness for the waxy smell of lemon polish these days, either.

Who knew an adrenaline junkie like him could fall for a bookworm gal like Evy? She read him like an open book. Which was fine by him.

Because aside from God, Evy Jane Shaw made everything true and right in his life.

Although he had a sneaking suspicion—occupational hazard—next time she might pick something like Tolstoy. At the thought, he bit back a groan. *War and Peace*. Seriously?

His parents agreed to park the RV until after the Christmas Eve wedding. Which couldn't arrive fast enough for him. His family welcomed Evy into the fold.

Including her chow mein noodle substitution for cornbread dressing. And Ursula Shaw's crème brûlée instead of his mother's usual pumpkin pie.

But hey, the crème brûlée, in his opinion, was spot-on. The Pruitt family Thanksgiving had gone forever international. And he for one couldn't have been happier about it.

His brothers pretended shock that Charlie could snare a gorgeous—and totally above his pay grade—woman like Evy Shaw. Didn't he know it.

Jokes erupted, via Skype and texts, about his impending nuptials, such as, "There's a new sheriff in town, and her name is Evy."

"Cell mates for life," Will teased earlier that morning. "Might as well laugh as to cry."

"Keep it up, Willster," Charlie threatened. "Your turn is coming, and I have a feeling I'll have the last laugh then."

But behind their ribbing, Charlie sensed their genuine regard for Evy.

He gazed around the dining room table. All the Pruitts had managed to phone home today. Jaxon and family, stationed in Europe. Ben, out at sea. Sister Anna from Texas.

Only Will, the never-serious brother, made it home for turkey this year. And leave it to Will somehow to elicit a chuckle from Evy's high-brow mother over cranberry sauce.

So many blessings. His family. A fulfilling job. His home.

And most especially Evy, his forever love. Charlie jumped up to help Evy clear the dinner table.

In the kitchen, he placed his hand at the small of her back. "I'm in over my head, Miss Shaw. I could use your help."

She smiled. "I'll wash, Deputy. You dry."

"But first…" He steered her out of the kitchen and into the study. "I meant I'm in over my head in love with you."

She laughed and snuggled into his embrace. "I'm never too busy for a library patron like yourself."

"I'm a work in progress, remember?"

"Aren't we all?" she teased.

"I'm going to need a lot of tutoring. A lifetime of it."

"That, Charlie Pruitt, will be my pleasure." She patted the window seat cushion.

He feigned outrage. "You're marrying me for this reading nook, aren't you?"

"That among other things."

"Prove it. What other things?"

She tilted her head. "Always got to prove everything with you. But if you must know…here goes my last secret."

"Last secret, huh?" He smiled. "No more secrets between you and me. After all, I've taken an oath to serve and protect."

"Seems like I've heard that line before, Deputy." She looked at him over her glasses. "But it'll be worth the wait, I promise." Her hand edged toward the glasses.

He beat her to the punch, pushing her glasses higher on the bridge of her nose with his index finger. "How about giving me a hint? Please?"

She fluttered her lashes. "You'll have to carry on as best you can, because I'm afraid you can't see me in my dress until the wedding."

"Now that…" His lips brushed across hers. "That is a secret worth waiting for."

And it was.

* * * * *

Dear Reader,

As soon as I turned in *Coast Guard Sweetheart* to my wonderful editor, Melissa Endlich, she said, "You've got to bring Sawyer and his sister together again." And so, two books later, I have.

Readers often ask whom I model characters upon. My characters aren't based on just one person, but an amalgamation of several people from whom I borrow certain physical or emotional characteristics to create a wholly fictional "person." There is also some truth to the idea that there is a little part of the author in each character, as well.

Like Evy, I've loved books since before I could read. One of my great childhood memories is finally getting my own library card when I was five years old. I still remember the first book I checked out—*Thumbelina*. The library has always been a haven for me. I get a happy feeling wandering among the stacks.

When I was in the sixth grade, I had a friend named Tina. She and her brother were living with their grandmother after the death of their parents. When Tina's grandmother died, she and her brother were sent to separate foster homes. I will never forget the sadness and fear on Tina's face their last day together at our school.

I never saw or heard from Tina again. I've always prayed that she and her brother found each other one day. And so was born Evy and Sawyer's story.

The theme of this book is wounded hearts. Is there a balm that can soothe hurting souls? There is—and His name is Jesus. It is the love of God and the blood of Christ that makes the wounded whole.

I hope you have enjoyed taking this journey with me, Charlie and Evy. I would also love to hear from you. You may email me at lisa@lisacarterauthor.com or visit www.lisacarterauthor.com.

Wishing you fair winds and following seas,
Lisa Carter

REQUEST YOUR FREE BOOKS!
2 FREE WHOLESOME ROMANCE NOVELS
IN LARGER PRINT
PLUS 2
FREE
MYSTERY GIFTS

༄ ༄ ༄ ༄ ༄ ༄ ༄ ༄ ༄ ༄ ༄ ༄ ༄ ༄ ༄ ༄ ༄ ༄ ༄

HEARTWARMING™

✿ ✿ ✿ ✿ ✿ ✿ ✿ ✿ ✿ ✿ ✿ ✿ ✿ ✿ ✿ ✿ ✿

Wholesome, tender romances

YES! Please send me 2 FREE Harlequin® Heartwarming Larger-Print novels and my 2 FREE mystery gifts (gifts worth about $10). After receiving them, if I don't wish to receive any more books, I can return the shipping statement marked "cancel." If I don't cancel, I will receive 4 brand-new larger-print novels every month and be billed just $5.24 per book in the U.S. or $5.99 per book in Canada. That's a savings of at least 19% off the cover price. It's quite a bargain! Shipping and handling is just 50¢ per book in the U.S. and 75¢ per book in Canada.* I understand that accepting the 2 free books and gifts places me under no obligation to buy anything. I can always return a shipment and cancel at any time. Even if I never buy another book, the two free books and gifts are mine to keep forever.

161/361 IDN GHX2

Name	(PLEASE PRINT)	

Address		Apt. #

City	State/Prov.	Zip/Postal Code

Signature (if under 18, a parent or guardian must sign)

Mail to the **Reader Service:**
IN U.S.A.: P.O. Box 1867, Buffalo, NY 14240-1867
IN CANADA: P.O. Box 609, Fort Erie, Ontario L2A 5X3

HW15